Valentino, Be Mine

Also by Tina D.C. Hayes

ROCK CANDY ROMANTIC SUSPENSE
Nefarious

PETAL PUSHERS MYSTERY SERIES
Poison, Perennials, and a Poltergeist
Secrets, Snapdragons, and a Spirit
Grudges, Goldenrods, and Ghosts

Novellas
No More Tears

Short Stories
"Midnight Reveille"

Valentino, Be Mine

Tina D.C. Hayes

Hazy Moon Ink

Copyright © 2016 by Tina D. C. Hayes.

Cover photography by Brittany Hayes
Cover modeling by Wonderland's Little Miss Scarlett Ida Clair

ISBN-13: 978-0692594988
ISBN-10: 0692594981

Hazy Moon Ink

Chapter One

Kaylee Rose huffed as she stood in line for what seemed like two hours, even though she'd only walked into Starbucks ten minutes before. The coffee shop wasn't usually this crowded on Sunday mornings, but some kind of convention was in town and by the looks of it, everyone was trying to get their caffeine fix before heading back to wherever they'd come from. The accents she heard suggested the other customers hailed from New York, Massachusetts, and Canada, and she was pretty sure the guy in front had an Irish lilt when he'd ordered his cappuccino.

Of all days. She'd stayed up late the night before to finish reading a romance novel, and with a full day ahead of her, she really needed her coffee spiked with a double shot of espresso. She was supposed to be across town to open the candle shop in fifteen minutes.

A glance at her watch made her huff again. Not only were the out-of-towners crowding the place, their orders either confused the barista or half the people behind the counter were new. Lattes were doled out at a snail's pace and being sent back for corrections twice as fast.

Only two more customers stood between her and the counter. Her caramel macchiato shouldn't take more than a minute or so for the person behind the counter to whip up. She really didn't want to be late. An important client was scheduled to come in before noon, and there was a good chance some of the convention crowd might stop by the shop on their way out of town.

The man with the Boston accent told the barista to have a wicked good day and grabbed a handful of napkins on his way out. Kaylee took another step toward the counter. A headache was forming behind her eyes and she desperately needed some strong coffee to ward it off.

Three more coffee craving customers rambled in. A cute guy and two women who looked like they should be on a street corner. From the way they were all cackling and carrying on, she guessed that unlike her, they were on their way home after a night of partying.

Kaylee shook her head and willed the line to move faster. She needed to buy her coffee and get to the shop. This was supposed to be a treat to wake her up, and she desperately did *not* want to overhear anything those three were talking about.

"What the heck?" Kaylee couldn't believe what she was seeing. The two bimbos stumbled to a seat while the guy with them walked up to the register as if nobody else was there ahead of him. No way was she going to stand by and let that jerk cut in front of her.

"Hey, the line ends over here."

The jerk was too busy flirting with the girl in the apron to hear her, apparently. He'd called Heather by name, so they either knew each other or he was intelligent enough to read her name tag. She had no idea why the girl behind the counter would want to talk to some drunk dude who stumbled in with two girlfriends, or whatever their situation was. Kaylee did *not* want to know the particulars of *that*, especially not on an empty stomach. She needed her caffeine, dang it.

"Hey," Kaylee said louder. She wasn't a confrontational person, under normal circumstances, but this wasn't a good day to cross her. No sleep, no coffee, not to mention all the crap she'd had to deal with these past six months.

The last thing she was going to tolerate right now was some playboy cutting the line to make her wait even longer to get served. Heck no. "You, up there, flirting with the barista. I said the line starts back here." She pointed at the floor behind her, in case the drunk needed more direction.

The two girls he'd walked in with cackled at that, which only made Kaylee madder. She had no intention of being laughed at by the likes of them.

The other barista gave the man in front of her his order. Now Kaylee stepped up to the counter, glaring at Heather in a way that suggested she better take her order, right then, or else. "I need a venti soy caramel macchiato with two extra espresso shots."

Heather rushed off to fill the jerk's order instead.

"Some of us have to go work," Kaylee said, sneering at the line breaker. "We don't all have the luxury of partying until the sun comes up." She paused to shoot a pointed glance at the two women he'd come in with. "Too busy doing God knows what all night to realize or care that you don't have the right to cut in front of everyone else. You need to get a job." She started to say he should get vaccines to guard against venereal diseases, but wasn't sure those shots existed. And her anger was aimed at him, not the sleazy girls he'd waltzed in with. "Go to work instead of hitting the bars so hard, and learn how to treat people with a little common courtesy. You smell like whiskey."

The jerk leaned back with his elbows on the counter. The seductive grin he flashed when he looked her up and down made Kaylee pretty sure he was still drunk from his all-night bender. "I've got a job, Miss Know-it-all. I'm a bartender."

Kaylee snorted in disgust. "That figures."

The barista slid three cups across the counter to him. "On the house." The coffee girl looked at the jerk like she wanted to lick whipped cream off him. Kaylee was about to explode. This was so not the day to tick her off.

The guy whispered something to the barista that made her turn red and giggle like an eighth grader. He turned around and spoke to Kaylee as he walked past her. While he stared at her chest. "You should come by Bourbon's Bar & Grill sometime, if you can tear yourself away from work long enough. First drink is on me."

He sauntered out with the two floozies before she could think of a fitting comeback. Darn straight any drink he ever bought her would be on him. She'd pour it over his insolent head.

She couldn't stop glaring at the jerk as he walked outside with his skanky drinking buddies. She almost gagged when he climbed into a flashy sports car, but then stifled a laugh instead. Romeo must be lacking somewhere in the manhood department, to feel the need to overcompensate with a hotrod like that.

Under Kaylee's intense glare, Heather bustled to make her caramel macchiato. Apparently, only gorgeous drunks who came in on the tail end of their buzz got comped with free java. Kaylee had to pay seven bucks for the privilege of being sober and waiting in line twenty minutes.

Her cell buzzed while she stomped to her car, cussing under her breath. She fished it out of her purse, then took a deep breath to try and calm down before she answered it.

A glance at the screen showed Pamela Fairbanks to be the caller. Thank goodness it wasn't her ex. She probably wanted her to dog-sit this weekend.

"Hi Pamela," Kaylee said as she got into her car. Her anger still wasn't completely under control. She slammed the door before she started the engine.

"Hi there, Kaylee. So glad I caught you this morning." Pamela lived down the street. Kaylee met her one morning when Pam was walking her Yorkie and

Kaylee was trying to walk off her stress overload. Both women were too caught up in their own thoughts to pay attention to where they were headed, so when their paths crossed, they bumped into each other. The little dog bit Kaylee's ankle, but when she laughed at the pup's funny expression instead of suing Pam for the superficial scratch, the ladies struck up a friendship of sorts that resulted in Kaylee dog-sitting whenever Pamela went out of town.

They made small talk before Pamela got to the reason she'd called.

"How would you feel about the possibility of keeping Valentino?"

"Sure, you know I love the little scamp." Kaylee meant it. The teacup Yorkshire terrier left a permanent impression on her heart right after he took a bite out of her ankle. "When do I pick him up, and how long will you be out of town this time?"

"No, I mean permanently. I got the promotion I told you about, but I have to move to Japan to take the position. I can't speak Japanese yet, but hey, I'm pretty psyched. Only problem is that I need to find a new home for Valentino. I just can't stand the thought of making him suffer in customs, since they have some quarantine regulations I don't want to put him through." Pamela sounded excited about the new job, but Kaylee wondered why she wasn't more upset about having to re-home her pet.

"So what do you say? Think you might be interested?"

Kaylee forgot all about the episode at the coffee shop as her mood took a turn for the better. The Yorkie would be a blessing, especially now, when her house felt so empty. When she dog-sat for Valentino, the rental home took on a different feeling. The dog had his flaws, like being way too spoiled for common sense, but he was sweet and loving. She had to tuck his little blue blankie around him at bedtime or he'd whine and look pitiful, but she loved to open her eyes on the mornings he was there and see him snoozing on the pillow beside hers. Valentino wouldn't lie or cheat or break her heart, unlike some roommates she'd had the misfortune of dealing with.

"Are you kidding?" Kaylee giggled as she pulled into the candle shop's parking lot. "That would be awesome! Thank you so much!"

"Great," Pamela said. From the labored breathing and the background noise, Kaylee guessed she was on a treadmill at the gym. "But before you get too excited, I need to let you know I haven't decided between you and another person. What I thought we'd do is let you and Carter take turns keeping Valentino for the next few weeks, swap him out every four days or so. That way we can all get a feel for who's better suited, and where the dog will be happiest."

"Oh." Kaylee tried to keep her spirits up despite her disappointment. "So we get a trial period?" While she'd like nothing better than to welcome the little dog into her home permanently, the last thing she needed was the added stress of auditioning to be a full-time pooper scooper. She had no idea who this Carter person was, but surely he or she couldn't outdo her on doggie care. If so, why would she have been the one in charge of watching Valentino every time Pamela left town? And how was Pamela going to decide the outcome of this anyway? Have her personal assistant stop by for home visits to make sure she cut Valentino's grilled chicken into small enough pieces?

"That's the idea. Hope that's okay." Pamela slurped some sort of drink, probably either a kale smoothie or that expensive imported water she liked so much.

"Sure, I guess." Since the woman was considering giving her the dog, she couldn't very well complain without sounding ungrateful. "When do we get started?"

They discussed the details as Kaylee unlocked the front door at the Flicker and Flame. Next week was the end of January, so Pamela wanted both prospective dog owners to get together with her personal assistant in a couple of days. That way Kaylee and Carter could meet and exchange contact information, since they'd be on their own as far as getting in touch with each other about when and where the exchanges would take place over the next month. The dog would stay with Kaylee the first four days and by the end of February, they'd know where the pooch would live permanently.

"Can you send me a list of everything I need to have on hand for Valentino? Latest favorite treats, all that stuff." She didn't need the ridiculous schedule Pamela kept him on; she'd seen enough of that when she pet-sat and figured that if she was going to be his new mom, they could both adjust to something more normal and less idiotic. A list of generic substitutes would be even better, but she knew better than to ask. Until a year ago, Valentino had starred in dog food commercials for a brand she was pretty sure the picky pooch would never have lowered himself to actually eat. When the company changed their spokesdog breed from Yorkies to French bulldogs, his original owner had given the pooch to Pamela, who he was dating at the time. They liked their dogs as spoiled as themselves and had spared no expense kissing his fuzzy little tushie. Kaylee, on the other hand, lived on a budget.

"Not to worry. I'm sending all his belongings with him. We'll divide it between you and Carter until we decide where he'll live permanently." Pamela must have finished her workout because she sounded more relaxed, her breathing back to normal, and soft music replaced the treadmill's hum. "I'll send along a PetSmart gift card to help with his upkeep during the transition."

They sat up a time before Pamela

hung up to hit the shower.

It was nice to have something to look forward to. Kaylee couldn't wait to take Valentino home with her, if not permanently, at least during the next month. With any luck, maybe she and this Carter person could strike up a friendship. Anybody who liked dogs couldn't be that bad, right?

Chapter Two

Wednesday morning, Kaylee woke up with a smile on her face fifteen minutes before her alarm went off. She absolutely couldn't wait to get to the park to meet with everyone, especially Valentino. After she ate a yogurt and fruit breakfast parfait, she dressed in jeans, boots, and a sweater. With her pockets full of the Yorkie's favorite peanut butter treats—the ones she bought at the pet store, not the mega-expensive brand Pam liked—she almost skipped out the door in anticipation of a wonderful day.

Winter temperature in western Kentucky could range from below freezing up to the rare sixties. After last week's snowstorm, the lower forties felt like spring had sprung, even though it would look more like it when the trees grew leaves and the ground wasn't covered with dead brown grass and sludgy mud puddles. Her jacket kept her warm as she walked through the park to meet Ruthie Lang, Pamela's personal assistant, the person responsible for bringing the dog and no telling how much canine paraphernalia. Dog food, as such, wouldn't be included, since Valentino was apparently too good for kibble and only dined on grilled chicken or fish mixed with organic steamed veggies. Pamela expected Kaylee to play chef when Valentino was in her care, but she really didn't mind.

Kaylee was the first to arrive at the bench near the deserted picnic tables. High-pitched yappy barks drew her attention before Ruthie rounded the path to join her. Valentino strained his harness at the end of the leash, leading the way, under his terms, just the way he liked it.

"Hi, Ruthie," Kaylee said before she bent down to greet her buddy. "How ya doing, boy?"

The little dog climbed onto Kaylee's bent knees to lick her face, his stubby little tail wagging away. He seemed content to let her hug him in her arms and then hold him in the crook of her elbow. She almost dug into her pocket for one of the peanut butter bones he liked so much, but decided against it, in case Ruthie Lang saw her feed him something that cost less than a million bucks. She didn't want to jeopardize her chances of keeping Valentino permanently.

"I left his gear in the car." The personal assistant plopped down on the park bench and rubbed her shoulder, which was probably sore from hauling all of Valentino's belongings around. "There's an Igloo filled with enough

19

free-range organic ingredients to last a good three weeks. Pam said you should still have the recipes, but I can always email them to you again if you need me to. All his little outfits, harnesses, leashes, and blankets are in totes. And don't worry, I packed all his toys, both of his crates, and picked up an extra car seat, so you'll each have everything you need."

"Thanks." Kaylee figured her trunk and backseat would be loaded to capacity by the time she strapped Valentino into his special car seat, which wasn't as frou-frou of a thing as she'd first thought. A teacup Yorkie that weighed less than four pounds wouldn't make it through a traffic accident without safety measures.

They sat on the bench to wait for Carter to join them. She hoped punctuality weighed somewhere in their evaluation, because whoever Carter was, he or she was fifteen minutes late the last time Kaylee checked her watch. Not that she minded. It was a little intimidating to meet the other potential owner. What if Valentino liked Carter better?

As if he sensed her worry, the Yorkie wiggled around in her arms and licked her cheek again. She draped him over her shoulder, a position she knew from experience that he enjoyed, and nuzzled her cheek against him.

Something behind Kaylee caught Ruthie's attention. A silly grin twisted her mouth as she threw her hand up in an exaggerated wave. Unless this Carter person was a complete moron, they were pretty hard to miss, since they were the only people in that part of the park.

"Carter, over here!" Ruthie stood and flapped her arms even more.

OMG. Either Pam's personal assistant had finally lost it after years of dealing with her perfectionist boss or there must be a celebrity walking up behind them. Kaylee was afraid to look.

She racked her brain for any movie stars named Carter but couldn't come up with a single one. From the blush on the other woman's face, she was pretty sure Carter was a man, and if not a famous one, he must be drop dead gorgeous.

Valentino's tail wagged in Kaylee's face as he barked his hello and squirmed against her shoulder. A masculine laugh sounded before Carter greeted them. "Good morning, Ruthie."

Kaylee ran her hand through her hair and pushed a section of bobbed blonde locks behind her ear before she turned around to meet him.

Sunglasses hid his eyes, but she could definitely understand why the PA was acting like a teenage girl backstage at a One Direction concert. Carter was smoking hot.

"Hey, dog, you glad to see me, boy?" His voice was even handsome, in a whiskey smooth kind of way. "May I?"

"Sure," Kaylee answered, and let him

hold the pooch that was squirming to get to him.

Then Carter took off his shades.

"You!"

It couldn't be, and she hoped to high heaven it wasn't who she thought. But it was. When he smirked at her, it erased any lingering doubt.

"I didn't know they let workaholics in here. Shouldn't your perky little nose be against a grindstone somewhere?"

Kaylee didn't care how gorgeous Carter was, she couldn't stand him. This was the last rung on her ladder of bad luck.

She huffed, but restrained herself from stomping her foot like a toddler having a tantrum. "Shouldn't you be getting home now that the sun's up, nursing another hangover with your harem of floozies?"

"I take it the two of you know each other?" Ruthie's widened eyes darted from Kaylee to Carter.

"You could say that." Kaylee made

an effort to reign in her anger. She'd heard somewhere that dogs picked up on emotions and she didn't want to upset him. "This guy stumbled into the coffee shop fresh off a bender, in questionable company, cut in line in front of me and flirted with the barista until he made me late for work. And he didn't even have the decency to apologize, even though I had to wait half the morning for my macchiato."

Amusement played in Carter's eyes as he listened to her. He scratched the dog behind the ears during her tirade.

"Your fussy friend is leaving out the part about her being so uptight and grumpy." Carter sat Valentino down on the bench. "I did invite you to come into the bar where I work for a free drink."

"Gosh, you're creepy. Give my drink to your flavor of the week."

"Okay, perhaps you two got off on the wrong foot." Ruthie had stood up as they squabbled, as if she might need to jump in the middle to separate them. "I know you're both good people, so we need to just let go of whatever happened the other day. Water under the bridge." When they both looked skeptical, Ruthie added, "We do have Valentino's best interest to think about, and it won't be good for him to hear the most important people in his life argue like this every time you get together."

Ruthie was right. Kaylee knew it and thought the jerk realized it too, since his downcast eyes made him look like a scolded schoolboy.

They both mumbled "fine."

"Okay then. Kaylee Rose, meet Carter Hartley." Ruthie gestured from one to the other during her somewhat formal introduction. "Carter, Kaylee. Now, you two shake hands and be friends."

Before either of them moved, Valentino sat down on the bench and raised one paw, barking to get their attention.

Since the dog was trying to follow Ruthie's command to shake, the others followed suit. Both petted the pooch at the same time, then stepped in to shake each other's hands.

The forced grin fell off Kaylee's face. "Is that beer I smell?" Her nose turned up. After Ruthie's attempt to get them to be civil, Kaylee tried to keep her voice inquisitive rather than argumentative. "Have you already been drinking this early in the morning?"

Ruthie frowned at that remark. She took a step closer to Carter and sniffed.

Before either woman could further chastise him, he shook his head.

"No, of course I'm not drunk at this time of day." Carter caught Kaylee's smirk and reworded his answer. "Or drinking at all. Beer must have spilled on my jacket last night when I moved some kegs around." When Kaylee rolled her eyes, he added, "At work. Geez, is she going to insist I take a breathalyzer test?"

Based on their first meeting and his apparent lack of morals, Kaylee didn't believe him. She didn't think the guy should be entrusted with a goldfish or the responsibility of watering plants, much less given the opportunity to take care of a somewhat delicate little dog. She narrowed her eyes at him. At least he had four days to sober up before his first turn with Valentino. She was glad to know that Pamela had the dog microchipped, in case this moron lost him, and that he was current on his shots. Heaven only knew what Carter's home environment must be like. She pictured women's underwear strewn around beat-up furniture in a room filled with empty liquor bottles and beer kegs.

"No, you could try to walk a straight line and say the alphabet, if you'd rather."

"That won't be necessary." Ruthie didn't appear to be entirely convinced, but it was obvious she was going to give him the benefit of the doubt. "I'm sure you won't smell of booze the next time you see each other. Which reminds me." Ruthie reached into her purse and withdrew two envelopes. "These have your contact information in them, so you can let each other know if anything comes up. Carter, where do you want to meet Kaylee Sunday, when it's your turn to have Valentino?"

He thought about that for a minute before he answered, the upturned corner of his mouth suggesting he'd almost opted for something witty, and possibly obscene, or so Kaylee suspected. "Would the ice cream parlor on Oak Street be alright, around three o'clock? It's dog-friendly so we can sit inside. Val likes French vanilla."

"Is ice cream on his approved food list?" Kaylee doubted it. He wasn't allowed to eat hotdogs and even his apple slices had to be organic.

"Pammy said it was fine once in a

while."

OMG. Did he just call Ms. Fairbanks *Pammy*?! Pamela would *sooo* freak out if she heard him refer to her that way. Oh no. A worse thought hit. What if Carter was *doing* ole Pammy? That's the only reason she could come up with for his being in the running for the dog. Gross!

A gagging sound effect poured out of Kaylee's mouth before she could stifle it. She pretended to choke on thin air instead, which must have been really believable.

Ruthie raised an eyebrow and patted her on the back. Kaylee figured she was lucky not be subjected to the Heimlich maneuver after her bad choking act. "Is that okay with you? To meet for ice cream?"

"Sure. That's fine." She cleared her throat, pretending to catch her breath after her attack. "I need to get to work."

They walked back to where their cars were parked and Ruthie opened the trunk so they could get the dog's gear.

Kaylee held Valentino in one arm and hefted two tote bags onto her opposite shoulder. She reached for the cooler, but Carter picked it up instead.

"I'll help you with that." Kaylee followed behind Carter, irritated at herself for imagining his muscles rippling underneath his denim jacket. She still thought he was an irresponsible jerk, but at least he had manners enough to move the cooler for her, and he wasn't too hard on the eyes. But that's as far as she'd ever let her imagination take her, as far as Carter Hartley was concerned. She had no intention of wasting her time on an alcoholic playboy.

Chapter Three

The joint was jumping for a weeknight. Behind the bar, Carter added butterscotch schnapps to apple pucker and vanilla vodka, put on the lid, and gave it a shake. He tossed the shaker in the air before he poured caramel apple martinis for two regulars who appreciated man candy skilled at mixing their drinks.

Too bad Kaylee wasn't open to his charms, the little prude. He pegged her for the type that would have to put on rubber gloves before she scooped up behind the little dog in her charge. He understood that cutting in front of her hadn't been the most polite thing to do the other day, but big whoop if she had to wait an extra fifteen seconds to get her coffee, some pretentious special order laced with soy. And today she'd apparently thought he was a raging alcoholic without enough common sense to look after a dog.

Anyway, he welcomed the idea of keeping Valentino, partly because he reminded Carter of the Chihuahua his mother had when he was little. He'd grown attached to the Yorkie when Pamela Fairbanks brought him to the bar, and had often looked after him while she schmoozed over drinks with colleagues and clients as she climbed the corporate ladder.

Carter certainly wasn't a lonely man, but he could get used to having the Yorkie around, as a buddy and a side-kick.

His dream of owning his own business wasn't that far away. He'd been managing Bourbon's Bar and Grill for nearly four years, and with the owner getting on in age, he was pretty sure he could buy the bar in the next year or so. He planned to remodel the place, aiming to keep his regulars while attracting a larger crowd with live bands and upscale food, rather than the current burger and fries special. Since Valentino once held a career as the face of Yummly dog food, Carter thought it would be cool to make him the bar mascot, have him star in commercials with a couple leggy models. The little dog enjoyed spending time behind the bar with him and could even do a few tricks, like trotting down the counter to fetch bar tabs in a little basket.

He'd be surprised if the pretty blonde chick would bother to pull herself away from her precious job, doing whatever it was she did, to spend time with the dog. He hoped she wasn't leaving Val in his crate for long hours while she was away, because that might break the spunky dog's spirit. Not that the know-it-all would listen to any advice that came from him. He hoped it wouldn't take long for Kaylee to get tired of waiting on Valentino so he could come live in Carter's apartment over the bar. That would be best for them all.

Carter looked forward to spending time with the dog. A Kentucky Wildcat dog bed waited upstairs in his living room, as well as a matching UK t-shirt in extra small. The cook was used to whipping up grilled chicken meals on Pam's request and had already cooked and frozen enough portions to last the little dog a month of Sundays.

The only thing about the arrangement that really rubbed him the wrong way was Pamela. He had misjudged her by a long shot. She'd been generous with tips, especially on nights Carter took the dog on potty walks for her, and he appreciated that. He had thought she was an overprotective dog owner who spoiled Val because she loved him so much. The thing was, that was totally wrong. How could anybody devoted to the dog just up and give him away? Yeah, she pulled the selfless card when she told him about not wanting the pooch stuck in customs, but he was pretty sure there were ways around that. The more he thought about it, he was starting to believe she'd spoiled the dog to her own whims rather than his own, and that she considered the Yorkie to be an accessory to her lifestyle.

Not much he could do about that, though it sure sucked for the pooch. But at least Pammy was trying to give him a good home. What she was thinking when she put Kaylee in the running, he had no idea.

Valentino woke Kaylee up a little

past midnight and scared her half to death. He was going bat-poop crazy, barking like his life depended on it. Then he leaped off the bed, dashed across the room, hopped up on a chair, and tried to paw his way through the window, all while snarling and barking his little head off.

Kaylee peeped out to see what had him all riled up. A man who lived a few doors down was out for a late night run after working the late shift. He'd stopped and it looked like he was trying to stretch a cramp out of his leg, but he'd stepped onto her front lawn to do it. Apparently, Valentino didn't like strangers in his new territory. Maybe he was afraid the guy was going to take a leak on his favorite oak tree. Who knows. Kaylee picked up the dog and tried to calm him down, but he kept on acting like a basket case until the guy set back off on his jog. He might be a teacup Yorkie, but he was as fearless as a Rottweiler. Kaylee didn't have to worry about anyone sneaking into her house unannounced.

The next morning, Valentino trotted into the Flicker and Flame like he owned the place. Whenever Kaylee had dog-sat in the past, she brought him to work with her. There wasn't too much he could get into at the candle shop, and he seemed to like sitting on the armchair with the purple cushion, like it was his personal throne from which to rule his Yorkshire kingdom.

Kaylee had opened the Flicker and Flame about two-and-a-half years ago, not long after she'd met her ex-fiancé. More functional than fancy, the building had previously housed a barber shop. The store was small but adequate, with a small shampoo room she'd converted into a workshop for making candles.

The rent was relatively cheap, but she had taken a sizable loan for her start-up costs, which included money for her to live on for the month before the store opened so she could build up her inventory of hand-crafted candles. The store also carried a very nice selection of candle holders, and she had a few shelves in one corner where she let local artisans display their wares. Last year business had done well enough for her to hire an employee full time, which had made her life a heck of a lot easier. Candles were her passion, not ringing up sales on the register. With Ben up front tending to customers, she was free to spend the majority of her time in the back, experimenting with new scents and playing with melted wax. Plus she could leave the shop in his capable hands whenever she needed to run an errand, set up at a craft fair, or like last fall, when she'd had to take two days off with the stomach flu.

Production amped up even more after she called off her engagement. Popularity had been low on her priority list since then. A good thing, considering most people from her social circle had been banished from her life along with her cheating ex and someone she'd thought was a good friend. Who needed to be surrounded by backstabbers, anyway? Between her sister, niece and nephew, Ben at work, and now Valentino, she had all the support she needed.

She had admittedly turned into something of a workaholic over the past six months. Pouring herself into her job held several benefits. Working to the point of exhaustion gave her a better chance of actually falling asleep instead of staring at her ceiling until the sun came up. The surplus inventory generated from all the extra hours she'd put in led her to expand sales through social media. Customers subscribed to her newsletter to get the scoop on upcoming sales events and special offers, and she'd opened new sales avenues in addition to the Flicker and Flame website, including Etsy, eBay, Facebook, Instagram, and Twitter accounts. She'd learned how to drown out emotional thoughts about people who weren't worth her time and grief by focusing on better, more inventive ways to make and market her product.

With Valentino in her lap, Kaylee sat down at the computer to check her email and any orders that had come in overnight. The dog wouldn't be still, so she gave up. She opened her desk drawer and took out a small red rubber ball with jingle bells inside it. The Yorkie hopped onto the floor and spun two circles, then waited for her to toss it for him. He loved to play fetch.

He eventually settled down to play with one of his stuffed toys, this time his little sock monkey dressed as a ladybug. Kaylee smiled at him. There was just something magical about having small children and dogs around.

The past few days with Valentino were the first time in a long while that Kaylee actually had fun. She got up early enough to walk Valentino down the street and around the block, an activity she repeated after dinner each night. Since she had to cook for the canine, she doubled the recipes and ate with him. In the living room on the couch, since she wasn't nutty enough to set a plate at the table for the d-o-g.

Just having Valentino beside her while she relaxed on the sofa was one of the best perks to his companionship, that and having him snuggle next to her as they slept. They vegged out watching reality TV each night, something she'd rarely had time for when she'd been throwing herself into her work.

She dreaded having to hand him over to Carter.

Kaylee would have preferred practically anybody short of Charles Manson to be Valentino's other prospective parent. Unfortunately, that wasn't her decision, just like the outcome of this trial period was out of her hands. She

41

had no other choice but to suck it up and deal with it, whether Carter got on her nerves or not.

Just the thought of Carter Hartley looking after Valentino made her nauseous. What use would he have for a pet, anyway? His shiny red sports car should be enough of a babe magnet. Surely he'd back out after he found out how much responsibility comes with being a pet owner. She figured she'd only have to be around the jerk a handful of times when they got together to exchange the dog, *if* he stuck it out until the end of February. Still, she knew she'd worry herself sick each time poor little Valentino was in his care, out of her sight.

What the heck could Pamela have been thinking?

Chapter Four

Monday afternoon was there before Kaylee knew it. She kissed the top of Valentino's furry head. He had a grooming appointment coming up in a couple of weeks, but since the little scamp liked to run around under the furniture, his 'do looked a total hot mess. Kaylee figured it would be a piece of cake to fix his hair. She could French braid her little niece's hair and was on her way to conquering the fish-tail, so how hard could it be to put a simple ponytail on the top of a Yorkie's head?

Like enduring the torment of Hades,

quite honestly. She had to get the hang of it because no way was she going to jeopardize her chances of keeping the dog by taking him into public looking like something a stray cat coughed up.

"Come on, Valentino, please be still." He wasn't having it. He must have had to endure getting his hair done when he was in commercials, but apparently, he was over that now. Kaylee had to restrain him, gently, with her knees on either side of his squirming body while she held his head as still as possible and brushed his hair. When she finally got the minuscule elastic wrapped around his topknot, she turned him around to make sure it was centered on his head.

It was. But unfortunately, the Yorkie could not blink.

Kaylee couldn't help laughing. Poor thing looked like he'd had one doozy of a facelift, due to his topknot being too tight. Not only could Valentino not blink his eyes, but his lids were also stretched open, giving him the appearance of a cartoon character. When the elastic came out, he shook his head before he shot her a disapproving look.

Hair stood out on his tiny head in all directions. Kaylee laughed harder because her little love bug looked like a ticked off version of Albert Einstein.

She redid the 'do, looser this time, though extra white still showed in the outer corner of his left eye. A few YouTube videos later, Kaylee knew the trick. Using the end of a rat tail comb, she inserted in very carefully under the hair between the new topknot and his peepers and used it to leverage a little bump of fur. With the Yorkie now coiffed and able to blink, she just had to add the bow. Happy with how he looked, she spritzed him with doggie cologne spray.

"Let's see you top that, Mr. Drunken Playboy."

In his red harness sweater that said 'Stud Muffin' in sparkly lettering, she took him for another potty walk around the block before they got in her car. She tossed the tote bag with his clothes, toys, and extra harness in the front floor board and as she strapped Valentino into his canine car seat, her heart sank down to her stomach. He licked her hand, his eyes dancing as if he expected her to take him for another jaunt through the park. Instead, she was duty bound to deliver him into the hands of a moron.

Kaylee eased her car into the parking spot in the lot next to Perkin's Ice Cream Parlor. At least she didn't have to haul every last bit of his doggie belonging each time she and Carter had an exchange. Pamela's overindulgence had resulted in Valentino owning at least two of nearly everything. Kaylee only had to haul the tote bag filled with Yorkie couture and his harness and leash collection. That was heavy enough. She was glad she didn't have to unhook the car seat and hand that over, since it had been a pain in the butt to adjust to the perfect height for Valentino to see out the window as he rode along. She for dang sure didn't trust Carter to drive without one. A simple tap of the breaks would send an unsecured teacup Yorkie flying airborne into the dashboard.

That was the only reason she fought the tempting urge to let Valentino ride in her lap when she drove. When he stayed with her, she rarely sat down without the Yorkie crawling up in her lap or snuggling up beside her. Knowing the spoiled little fart, it was possible he only wanted to share her body heat, but she liked to think he wanted her company as much as she needed his. With the possibility of him becoming hers permanently in a few weeks, she couldn't help but grow more attached to him with each passing day. She truly loved the little scamp.

When she approached the back passenger side door and peeked inside to see Valentino standing with his paws on the side of his car seat, her heart melted. She realized, as she picked up the little dog and let him rest with his front paws on her shoulder, that this must be how divorced parents felt when they had to turn their small children over for custodial visits. Thank heavens she didn't have kids with her ex-fiancé.

"Good grief." She passed a red sports car parked in front of the ice cream parlor. "That figures." Carter had straddled the line to take up two spots when he'd parked. A sarcastic grin tugged the corner of her mouth. He must have the mistaken idea that everything he owned and prized was much bigger than reality suggested.

Carter stood up to greet them when they walked inside. With effort, he rearranged his face and forced a grin. They exchanged greetings as he took the tote from her shoulder and motioned for her to take a seat at the table.

"So." Carter was apparently making an effort to get along with her, or at least his manner and tone suggested as much. "How have you been? And how's Valentino adjusting to the situation?"

Kaylee couldn't pick up the slightest hint of an accent when he spoke. She found that a little odd. Everyone originated from somewhere, but he could just as easily be from Seattle as Tennessee or New York with his vanilla inflection. Kaylee was proud of her Kentucky twang and of the community she lived in. She'd been too irritated the other two times she'd been around him to notice the precise way in which he spoke. Carter sort of sounded like a radio announcer reading the evening news.

"We're both fine, thanks for asking." Kaylee would like to get along with Carter on these exchanges, but she thought it best not to let her guard

49

down. Civil, she could do. "There's not really much of an adjustment for Valentino to make, though. I dog-sit for Pamela every week or so, whenever she has to go out of town on one of her endless business trips." A bit of smugness set in since everything she was telling him was not only true, but it strongly hinted that the dog would be better off staying with her permanently. She tried not to gloat. "My place is like his second home."

"Well, I'm glad he's comfortable with you." If Carter picked up on the barb, he didn't show it. Perhaps he was as masterful at hiding his emotions as he was at stripping the flavor of his hometown from his voice. "I have to admit that I've been looking forward to having him stay with me, as well. He sure adds life to the place."

"He's a lot of fun to have around." So long as he was engaged in small talk, she might as well ask the question that had been on her mind. "I was wondering how you know Valentino."

He grinned at her. She hoped to high heaven that he wasn't about to tell her he got acquainted with the Yorkie when he had sleepovers with *Pammy* in some sick and twisted open relationship. The image of those two together, like that, made her want to gag.

"I met Valentino at the bar I manage." Carter leaned back in his chair. He wore a short sleeved t-shirt despite the cold weather, probably to show off his killer biceps. Kaylee tried her best to ignore his muscles as he spoke. "Pammy was at one of the tables on the patio one afternoon last summer. Valentino sat in her lap, until a stray cat walked by. This little dog shot out like a cannonball chasing that cat down the street, hell-bent on catching a tomcat that weighed at least twice his weight."

"Oh no." Kaylee's heart raced just thinking about poor Valentino running down a crowded road with traffic buzzing past him. She couldn't bear to think about what could happen if he stepped in front of one of those tires. "I know from experience he's not easy to catch. Please tell me he stayed out of the street."

"I would, but I'd be lying." Carter brushed his hand through his dark curly hair. "I saw him take off, so I chased after him. He may be small, but that dog can run fast when he's motivated. The cat climbed up a tree when Valentino closed in on him, which is the only reason I caught him. He was so proud of himself, yapping away, looking up at that cat he'd treed." A dimple appeared beside Carter's lips when he grinned.

"So, after that, Pammy asked me to watch him sometimes when she met clients and co-workers at the bar. If her colleague was a dog person, she'd keep Val in her lap. Otherwise, she'd ask me to entertain him or walk him around the block a few times to do his business. One man was actually afraid of Valentino, if you can imagine that."

"Really?" Kaylee liked this side of Carter much better, but she still didn't intend to let her guard down, no matter how much his blue eyes sparkled. "How could anybody be afraid of this?" She gestured to the pooch in her lap. "No offense, Valentino."

"I'm serious. He was a big guy, too. Muscled up like a football player. A waitress walked through with a tray full of bacon-wrapped appetizers, so Val barked at her, trying to demand a treat." His grin widened as he reached out to pet the dog she held. "His barking actually scared the guy. He jumped up and backed away like he was afraid he'd get bitten. I had to laugh, couldn't help it. Anyway, I let the Yorkie put in some time tending bar with me that afternoon."

Some teenagers sat down a few tables away and dug into banana splits. Valentino stood up in Kaylee's lap, his paws on the arm rest as he watched. The dog licked his lips and let them know what he wanted. He aimed his first bark at Kaylee, then another in Carter's direction. He would have jumped down and tried to talk the kids out of a few bites if Kaylee hadn't had him under control.

"If you'll excuse me a moment, I'd better go get him a scoop or we'll never hear the end of it." He patted Valentino on the head before he walked to the counter.

Kaylee checked her cell while he was ordering. If Ben Pratt got bored when left in charge of the candle shop, he'd text her silly questions about what to do in situations that would never in a million years come up. What should he do if someone allergic to wax wandered in and collapsed from anaphylactic shock? How many bees did it take to make a beeswax candle? That sort of thing. But hey, the guy was a dependable employee and fun to be around.

Since he hadn't sent a message, she guessed he must be busy selling her candles to happy customers.

"Here we go." Kaylee looked up when Carter returned to the table with a tray loaded down with ice cream. She hoped he didn't expect the little dog to eat all of it. "May I?" Carter reached for Valentino.

"Sure."

Carter hugged the pooch before he sat him down on the table. The dog licked his lips as Carter slid his treat toward him. "One scoop of French vanilla for you, boy."

Valentino licked the ice cream with such enthusiasm that Carter moved the napkin dispenser to the center of the table, in front of the dish, to keep it from being pushed into the floor.

The tray held two more dishes. He slid one over to Kaylee and spooned mint chocolate chip ice cream into his mouth. "Yours is chocolate with caramel swirls."

55

"Thank you." Kaylee stared at hers as if the dog had taken a dump on it. It was sweet of him to think of her and she appreciated the gesture, but there was no way she could eat it.

Her spoon went untouched while Valentino and Carter noshed on their ice cream.

"Something wrong with yours?"

"No, it's just that . . . . I'm sorry, but I have a dairy allergy." Kaylee hated having to explain her condition, but she didn't want to look rude or un-grateful when he was actually trying to get along. "But it was nice of you to buy me a scoop."

Carter shot her a skeptical glare.

"So," Carter said, "you're allergic to the ice cream I bought you?"

She didn't owe this guy an explana-tion. Was the arrogant jerk actually ac-cusing her of lying about it? She took a deep breath and tried to quell the an-ger that slithered up the length of her spine. "I'm allergic to ice cream and

56

dairy products, yeah. Why, exactly, do you find that so hard to believe?" She pushed the cardboard dish across the table to him and crossed her arms.

"Just thought it was odd that you agreed to meet here," he said. "Around all this toxic rocky road."

She glared at him. No use trying to argue with someone this ignorant.

"Everybody has a condition these days. Gluten is probably the most ridiculous. Let a couple of celebrities say they're too delicate to digest wheat or whatever, and then the whole country comes down with the same thing. For a while." Carter rolled his eyes as he spooned more mint chocolate chip ice cream into his mouth. "So tell me, who among the famous are lactose victims this week?"

"Were you actually born this stupid?" Kaylee could not believe any educated person would say such things. But then again, considering the type of people he hung out with and his hobby of choice being beer pong, it wasn't that surprising. "I'm not being trendy or jumping on some fad diet. I was born with a dairy allergy. And do you have any idea how hard it is for little kids to steer clear of ice cream at parties and school functions? Especially with the world full of morons like you?"

Kaylee's niece was used to eating frozen vegan treats and had trouble understanding that dairy products that looked the same were not the same. Just last month, Natalee had gone to a birthday party and even though her mom had explained her allergy to the parents in charge, she got a call to come pick her up early because she was so sick. The other mom said Natalee really wanted one of the ice cream cones like the other kids had, and she hadn't thought just one would hurt anything. She even got defensive and asked why Natalee would eat something that would give her violent stomach cramps and make her vomit.

Kaylee wondered if that idiot was related to Carter.

"Oh, I get it. I'm the moron, but you're the one who's too good to take my peace offering." Carter kept his voice cool but shook his head. "That's fine. Valentino can have yours. He appreciates my kindness."

Carter put the chocolate ice cream in front of Valentino, who had just finished the last of his special French vanilla scoop.

"Are you crazy!" Kaylee snatched the bowl off the table and slammed it into the nearest trash can. She sat back down, then pulled Valentino protectively against her chest.

"God, you're rude."

"Me! Don't you know chocolate is poison to dogs? And no, it's not because Valentino's being too trendy that if he eats chocolate, it could literally kill him. Google it if you don't believe me, but please, for heaven's sake, don't ever try to feed him anything like that again." The dog snuggled up closer to her. Kaylee couldn't stand the thought of anything happening to him. "Same goes for mushrooms and grapes. Didn't Pamela's assistant give you the no-no list?"

"Yes, but I haven't had a chance to look over it yet." Carter blinked and raised an eyebrow. "Sorry, didn't know, but I'll read it when we get home."

Kaylee wanted to ask if he was responsible enough to take care of the dog, but decided to choose her words carefully. "Are you sure you're going to be able to handle taking care Valentino by yourself? Do you have much experience with pets, other than taking this one on potty walks at a bar?"

He took a deep breath, then exhaled it slowly. "Okay, I should have read the instructions Ruthie gave me. My bad. I'll study the list this afternoon, I promise. I'm sure we'll be fine."

"Please call me if it gets to be more than you can handle. Please." Kaylee kissed the pooch on his snout. "I'll be happy to drop whatever I'm doing and run over to get him. Anytime, day or night." The last part she added after picturing Carter doing shots with a room full of strippers, and Valentino sitting in a vat of rat poison.

"I'm not incompetent." Carter sat up straighter and reached for the dog. "Pammy wouldn't consider giving Val to me if I was."

That brought her back to the cold hard reality of the situation. She had no choice but to hand the Yorkie over knowing he might very well end up living in a seedy bar with Carter. She shivered when Valentino left the safety of her arms.

"Can we meet up at the same time this Sunday, but at the mall?" Kaylee slung her purse over her shoulder as she stood up. She could not stomach being in this man's presence another second.

"That's fine. I can meet you in front

of Hot Topic." Carter surprised her by holding Valentino with his back in the crook of his arm, like a baby doll. Valentino didn't seem to mind the submissive position at all, especially not when he got a belly rub.

"See you there." Kaylee opened the door on her way out. His flashy sports car still straddled the parking line. She shook her head and said back over her shoulder, "Please drive carefully. Do *not* forget to use his car seat."

Tears stung her eyes as she stomped back to her car. Worry squeezed her heart. She was absolutely helpless to do anything about the situation, other than provide the best home for the Yorkie she could, and pray Pamela would recognize her as the more responsible and loving of the two.

Her car felt so empty without Valentino in the backseat.

Chapter Five

After a few minutes, Carter carried everything out to his car. Considering how full the dog's stomach must be from eating all his ice cream, he snapped a leash onto Valentino's harness and took him for a quick walk in the lot across the street. Valentino sniffed around before he watered three oak trees and left something special for the squirrels beside the roots.

He felt ridiculous putting a dog in a car seat, of all things. But Pam had made him promise after she'd explained how crushed she'd be if her precious Yorkie got hurt.

Carter started up his car and headed for home, his apartment over the bar. It was a pretty nice place to live, plus it came free with the management position. On the top floor of the building, the one bedroom apartment had a small living area and open kitchen. The breakfast nook beside the front window was more than enough dining space for a bachelor who had no interest in throwing dinner parties. He saved a fortune in gas since he didn't have to drive to work; all he had to do was get dressed and go downstairs, and there he was. The only drawback was that he couldn't call in sick unless he actually was, since the only way in or out of his apartment was through the bar below.

Not that he was tempted to blow off his job. His position as manager and bartender was fun for now and paid pretty well, but his dream of owning the place drove him to excel at work. He knew the current owner wanted to see the bar stay open and expand, not be sold out to some trendy burger joint or incense shop. When he'd saved enough money, and proven himself capable of running a successful business, he was pretty sure Jeff Owens would sell it to him. They'd discussed that very thing before.

Carter grabbed a bacon cheeseburger from the cook on the way up to his apartment. He knew the Yorkie usually ate his meal at noon, so he didn't get out the doggie dish. When the little furball stared up at him, he felt guilty, even more so when the dog reared up with his front paws on Carter's leg and whined, his little nose twitching as he smelled hot hamburger. He pinched off a piece of crispy bacon, then paused with it gripped between his fingers. He'd almost screwed up royally with the chocolate ice cream and didn't want to accidentally poison the dog.

"Hang on just a minute, boy." Carter chewed as he walked. He sat back down with the no-no list in his hand.

Bacon wasn't on there so he gave Valentino a few pieces, which he gulped down like a miniature starving wolf. Carter studied the paper while he finished his early supper. Most of the food on the list he never ate anyway, like grapes and macadamia nuts, but he'd have to remember not to let his tiny house guest have guacamole or bits of avocado that might fall out of a sandwich.

Valentino nosed around the floor beside the refrigerator as if he were looking for something. Carter filled a dish with water and set it down. Must have been what he wanted since he drank half of it, and got the long hair under his chin soaking wet. Carter probably needed to use a smaller bowl. For now, he just dried him off with a dish towel and snapped on his leash for one more walk before he went to his office. He needed to do some paperwork before he took over the bar for the night.

He tossed a rope bone onto the chair

in his office and set Valentino down to play with it. The dog turned two circles, then plopped down with the toy between his front paws.

When Carter stepped behind the bar later, there were only three customers in the place. About par for six o'clock on Sunday afternoon. Business would pick up around seven and taper off until closing at eleven. It was an easy pace, as opposed to Fridays and Saturdays when the bar didn't close until two a.m. and stayed busy from lunch until last call.

Carter chopped lemons and limes into wedges as Valentino played with some chew toys at his feet. The area behind the bar was closed off except on one end. Until he could get a gate or something to keep the dog corralled, he decided the best bet would be to leave his leash and harness on, with the handle looped over the lite beer tap.

A man in a Saints jersey ordered a Corona. Carter popped the cap, put a lime sliver in the bottle, and served the customer before he went back to prepping for later. The yellow and green fruit on the cutting board seemed to morph into Kaylee's blonde hair and jade eyes as their conversation from earlier replayed in his mind. He still thought she was rude to refuse the ice cream. His mother had raised him to eat whatever was put on his plate and to be grateful for it, whether he particularly liked the taste or not. He wasn't an idiot, but he thought she'd exaggerated her lacto thing just as an excuse to look down her pretty little nose at him. He'd be a rich man if he had a dollar for every time a girl he went out with ordered salad instead of real food under the pretense of a gluten problem, allergy, swearing off carbs, or not eating meat because of some new-fangled religion they supposedly followed; later he'd see those same girls scarf down things they didn't know contained said gluten and carbs, or the holy vegetarians noshing on a T-bone steak. The women he dated were superficial that way, with their worst nightmare being Instagrammed with a mouthful of anything that would make their butts look bigger.

Kaylee was a beautiful woman, but he knew her kind too well. Her Type A personality and perfectionist nature made her think she was better than everybody else, and he knew she looked down on him. Her cracks about booze were her way of downgrading his job bartending. He couldn't imagine anything more torturous than having to spend time letting her boss him around, which made him feel sorry for Valentino on his visits with her. But he was probably being too harsh. She did seem to love the pooch, the way she cuddled him up to her chest, and the way the dog licked her face and wagged his tail when she spoke to him showed that Val loved her right back, an emotion the dog didn't lavish on many.

Quite frankly, Val was snooty, a trait somehow inherited from Pammy. Carter had seen the dog refuse expensive gourmet treats from the ladies who flirted with him at the bar. The dog would turn up his nose and walk away, until Carter or Pamela offered him the exact same treat, which he'd then gobble up and lick his lips over.

A few more customers had come in, mostly people stopping by to relax with a drink after working through the weekend. He made a Manhattan for an older gentleman, a lawyer with an office in town. The dog yapped when Carter poured fresh mixed nuts in a bowl and set it on the bar beside the drink. He picked Valentino up and tried to explain that he didn't remember which kind of nuts he wasn't allowed to feed him. The dog squirmed, kicked, and lunged for the bowl the whole time. The lawyer laughed at the sight and then asked if he could hold Val.

Carter handed Valentino over. The older gentleman's face, usually haggard and distant, lit up when he touched the Yorkie. Since the picky pooch warmed up to him, he was probably a nice guy.

"Come say 'hi' to Bernie, boy, I won't bite." The lawyer laughed. "My daughter had one just like him when she was little. Named her Suzy-Q, and I never did know whether it was after the song or the lunch cake." Bernie nuzzled his face up to Valentino's, and actually looked a good twenty years younger with his big grin.

Long before last call, Valentino's new personal fan club settled around the bar to play with him. He ate up the attention, and even lowered himself to perform a few tricks he'd learned during his television days. Carter let him run up and down the bar to whichever patron called him over. Valentino dazzled them by shaking hands, giving high fives, and when Carter pretended to aim an imaginary gun at him and said 'bang-bang,' Val fell on his side and played dead. Until the applause died down. Then he stood up and literally took a bow. No telling how much his original owner had paid to have the little fart trained so well.

The only drawback to Valentino's stay was that Carter had to get out of bed at eight o'clock to take the dog out. The first morning he'd simply ignored the Yorkie when he climbed up on his chest, sat down, and whined every few seconds, waiting for the man in charge to open his eyes. He'd nearly laughed when the dog hopped off his bed and quit pestering him. When he did get out of bed later that morning, Valentino looked up from the stuffed toy he was chewing on long enough to give Carter a smug look as he walked past the couch.

On his way to the bathroom, Carter stepped in a warm pile of dog poop. He hobbled to the bathroom on one foot and the other heel, cussing the whole way until he scraped the mess off his toes, flushed it down the toilet, and took a quick shower.

He emerged from the bathroom toweling off his hair. "That was not cool, buddy."

Valentino made eye contact, spun in a circle, and barked back.

Carter never found the matching wet spot he was pretty sure Val left in his apartment. The dog didn't have much to empty out when he finally got his walk that morning.

Chapter Six

Valentino learned that if he jumped a certain way, he could make the opposite end of this leash fall off the beer tap it was secured to. One night of frantically searching the bar for a dog small enough to fit into the average purse was all Carter could stand. He acted like a crazy person, scared to death that the dog might get outside and dart into traffic or that someone might sneak off with him. Caring for Valentino was his job now, one he hoped to have permanently, and he almost upchucked worrying that something had happened to him. Carter offered a night of free drinks to whoever helped him find the Yorkie.

At one point, he ordered the bouncer to bar the front door until the dog turned up. Two customers exchanged worried glances, then the slightly intoxicated one said he had to get home before midnight or his wife would kill him. He downed another shot of tequila and said, "Screw it, she's a terrible shot anyway."

Finally, an elderly lady who came in each week after bingo held her hand in the air. "He's over here, I've got him!" Turns out the little scoundrel had hopped up in the booth beside her and tried to make a lunge for her cheese fries. Carter scanned his mental list and didn't think potatoes or cheese would necessitate getting his tiny stomach pumped. When he sprinted over to retrieve the runaway, the lady was hugging and kissing on Valentino, and feeding him cheese fries off a fork. Val had the gall to try to hide under the woman's shawl.

"I like sherry," the elderly lady said, smiling as she gave the Yorkie one final squeeze before handing him over. "And keep 'em coming. On the house, right, since I ratted this little fella out?"

"Yes Ma'am," Carter said. "Thank you. I'll get that sherry out in a jiff."

After that, Carter kept Valentino tethered to his wrist. It made for an embarrassing trip to the john, but he wasn't going to risk that sort of thing happening again on his watch. Carter didn't know how people lived through raising children without ending up in the looney bin from the stress of it all. He had a new found respect for his old college buddies who posted all those pictures of themselves with their kids. They deserved medals.

Valentino's first visit with Carter was over before they knew it. Carter gave the little dog a good once over before they left. No way did he plan to let Kaylee find anything to fault him with, not in his dog-care abilities or his personality either. "Come here, boy. You're looking kind of scruffy."

One glance at the brush in Carter's hand and the dog made a run for it. He darted under the table in the breakfast nook and barked to show that he had the upper hand. When Carter moved the chair and squatted down to pick him up, he was off like a streak of lighting to hide under the bed.

Carter finally pulled him out. Deep cleaning wasn't one of his strong suits, so Valentino was covered with dust bunnies. The pooch sneezed mid-squirm.

"Great. Why do I have the sneaking suspicion both you and Kaylee have dust allergies in addition to not being able to eat regular food like chocolate, ice cream, and guacamole." Carter held Valentino up in one hand and brushed him as best he could. The straight part that normally ran down the dog's spine was crooked, his blue hair bow sat askew, and clumps of dust still dotted his nose, ears, and feet. "No way I'm going to wrestle your little behind into a bathtub. But I've got an idea."

With the dog tucked under his arm like a glass football, Carter carried him to the kitchen sink. He grabbed a clean dish rag, dampened it with warm water, and used it to sponge off all the dust he saw. He rinsed it, wrung it out, and ran it over every inch of the protesting pooch. Then he had to fluff up his fur again with the brush. Valentino tried to play tough guy when he snarled at the brush and snapped at the handle, but Carter thought it was one of the funniest things he'd ever seen.

With a clean harness buckled on the dog and a leash attached, they went to the car and headed across town to the mall. Carter wondered if Kaylee worked so hard just to support a shopping addiction. He knew lots of beautiful girls who ran up credit card debt fueled by shopping sprees for shoes, clothes, Coach purses, and anything they found on sale at Macy's. Wouldn't be hard to tell. If Kaylee showed up loaded down with mall shopping bags, he'd have to make a snide comment about it to show her that nobody was perfect, not even her.

He made a mental note not to smart off until he'd asked about borrowing a baby gate.

Carter hit his blinker and turned his car into the mall parking lot. He headed toward a parking spot when some jerk in a beat-up Chevy almost backed into him. Before Carter knew what he was doing, he sat on the horn, stuck his head out the window, and yelled, "Hey buddy, watch where you're going! There's a teacup Yorkie in here!"

Valentino trotted beside him in a perfect heel. Carter had to walk slower than usual, with those short Yorkie legs keeping up. When he spotted a gang of nine-year-old girls coming out of Build-a-Bear, he scooped the dog up, and just in time. They rushed over and started oohing and aahing over the adorable pooch, six or seven affectionate little hands reaching to pet him all at once.

"Girls, let's give them a little breathing room." A redhead who bore a striking resemblance to the tallest girl rushed over. "Did you even ask if it was alright to pet his puppy?"

"That's okay, he enjoys the attention." Carter was proud of Valentino and sort of ate it up that the little girls recognized canine perfection when they saw it.

"He is awfully cute. May I?" She held out her hands and as if on cue, Valentino squirmed in her direction.

"Okay," Carter said, a bit reluctant to hand the dog over, but he didn't want to be rude. What could it hurt, and the dog really did like to show off. "Just please be careful not to let him get down." He did not hand over the

81

leash handle, to ensure the dog wouldn't get lost in the crowd even if he escaped the woman's grip.

The redhead nuzzled her face against Valentino's, then leaned over so the girls could get their doggie fix for the day. Unfortunately, the woman's shirt was a bit too low-cut. Valentino's hind leg kicked against her chest, and, well, she had a wardrobe malfunction.

Carter tried his best not to peek. She had to be a D-cup, so it wasn't easy for him to look away.

"Mom! Oh my gosh, cover up!" It was the tall girl, nearly in tears about her mother's overexposure. "What's wrong with you? You wouldn't even let me wear a tank top to school! Geez!"

Carter tried to grab the Yorkie. Not the best idea.

"Oh my goodness, Carter! What the heck are you doing?"

Carter squeezed his eyes shut. Only one person that voice could belong to. Under his breath, he said, "Kill me now."

The redheaded girl was still slapping at his hands.

"I am *sooo* sorry." Kaylee rushed over and took Valentino from the exposed woman's hands. In some girl-powered show of solidarity, she even tried to help the redhead pull up her V-neck to remedy the nip slip.

"Please, Mom, can we just go home?" The woman's daughter was thoroughly humiliated. Not much doubt this would be a topic of conversation in therapy sessions for her in years to come. "Just wait until I tell Dad about this."

The redhead didn't make eye contact with Carter, but thanked Kaylee for her assistance. Her daughter, however, sneered at Carter as if he were the porn king of the Western hemisphere as they walked past. The last he saw of them, they were headed into The Gap.

"Have you no shame?" Kaylee cradled Valentino against her chest and glared at Carter like she wanted him to spontaneously combust. "Did you not see those kids with her? I saw you grabbing at her t—"

"It wasn't what it looked like." Carter felt like a total perv. "I swear. Those little girls bum rushed Val and me. I was trying to be nice, to let them and their mom pet the pooch for a second, like they asked. Just hear me out."

Kaylee scanned the area around them. A couple of mall walkers whispered and pointed in Carter's direction, two young mothers pushed strollers past him at full speed as they pulled their necklines up to their chins, and one guy in a hoodie leaned back with a grin on his face, waiting to see what would happen next.

"Don't you think we should move on, you know, so the vice cops can't find you so easily?" Kaylee was the picture of indignation. When Carter reached for the Yorkie, she shifted him to her other shoulder.

"Fine." Carter handed her the leash

and tried to shrug off the pervy situation. "We could sit in the food court, if that's alright." He attempted to lighten the mood. "Promise not to try to make you eat any ice cream this time."

Kaylee nodded. She looked the dog over as if she thought he was lucky to be alive after four whole days in Carter's care. Good thing he'd run the brush over Val's coat and wiped off the dust before they came.

They walked in silence. Carter was glad when they were far enough away from the incident that people weren't still staring at him. A new conundrum hit when they arrived at the food court. He for damn sure wasn't going to sit at a table in front of a booth that sold ice cream, but with her dairy allergy, it was hard to avoid all the places that hawked lactose laden food. Most carried cheese of some sort, either featured in an entree or as an ingredient. Where the heck could she eat, anyway? Not that they were going to share a meal anytime soon, but still, it made him stop and wonder.

And after his faux pas at the ice cream parlor, he probably shouldn't sit close to the chocolate booth.

He opted for the only place he was pretty sure wouldn't offend her on any level. Salad in a Box.

"You know I'm not going to croak if I look at dairy products, right?" Kaylee sat down and rolled her eyes as she perched the Yorkie on her lap. "I don't want to eat it, either, but neither would any other sane person who gets sick from it." The hint of a grin threatened to emerge at the corner of her mouth. "It was considerate of you to think about it, though. My grandpa loves hot fudge sundaes and I make them for him whenever I visit. So long as it doesn't get in my mouth, I'm good."

"Okay. I just wanted to let you know that I'd like for us to get along, and I'm sorry for being a jerk the other day." Carter sincerely meant it. He did not apologize often, but when he knew he was in the wrong, he was honor bound to admit it and move on. "Valentino's no-no foods, as you call them, are all up here now." He pointed to his temple. "Memorized them as soon as I got home with the pooch."

"Good. Thanks." Kaylee visibly relaxed. "Please don't think I was judging you or anything. I guess we haven't been showing our best sides to each other." Her cheeks turned pink. "Okay, that's not exactly what I meant, especially considering that I walked up on you groping a woman in front of a bunch of little girls, but anyway, I wasn't trying to make you feel like you had to earn a gold star on your forehead."

"That, back there, was not what it looked like." Carter was glad to see that Miss Perfect had a vulnerable side, and wasn't always so uptight. "If you really thought it was, you wouldn't be sitting here with me now. Or you would've called the cops to report my lewd and lascivious behavior under the guise of talking to your BFF."

Her face clouded over. He mentally went over the words he'd just said and for the life of him, could not figure out how he'd managed to offend her this time.

After a quick cuddle with Valentino, she shook off whatever was bothering her. He hoped it wasn't his fault.

"Okay, what really happened? Tell me your side of the story, and I might just give you the benefit of the doubt." She peered at him with her big jade eyes in a way that made him not want to disappoint her.

"The little girls ran to us when they saw Valentino and instantly fell in love with him. That woman, one of their mom's, I think, came out of Build-a-Bear to apologize for the girls petting the dog without asking permission first. Maybe they'd talked about that in Brownies or something, I don't know, but she admonished them about it." Carter took a deep breath before explaining the worst part of it. "Then the mom asked to hold Val, so I handed him over. His foot got stuck in her, um . . . down her blouse, and when you walked up, I swear to God, Kaylee, I was trying to take the dog and help the lady cover herself up."

"Why was the one little girl slapping your hands away from her mom's bosom, and about to break out in tears?"

"She's a little kid, and to her, it was uber-embarrassing. She somehow misunderstood what was happening and thought I was grabbing her mom's, um, chest, instead of trying to help her pull up her shirt."

Kaylee's laughter thoroughly surprised him. He grinned in spite of himself.

"That does sound more believable, I hate to admit, than what it looked like when I walked up on you earlier." Kaylee leaned back in her chair and

Valentino laid his head down on her lap. He seemed to enjoy watching his new best buds interact without biting each other's heads off.

"Thanks, I guess." Carter grinned back at her. Then he noticed that she wasn't loaded down like a pack mule with mall shopping bags, like he'd assumed she'd be. "For understanding I was clumsy in an unfortunate situation. Really, though, where must your mind have been to jump to that other conclusion?" he teased.

"I like you much better this way." Kaylee's cheeks turned pink again. She looked beautiful.

"Hey, would you like to get something to eat?" He surprised himself, but he actually wanted to spend time with her. Valentino sure seemed smitten with his lovely blonde caretaker, as he snuggled into her lap. Carter liked her laugh and wanted to hear it again. "My treat?"

A screaming kid stole their attention.

A little boy who looked to be about eight years old was throwing some sort of temper fit in front of the taco booth. His mother tried to calm him down, but that only seemed to make things worse. An older lady walked up to help the woman quiet her son, but when she made the mistake of putting her arm around the boy, he totally lost it. He threw himself down on the floor, kicking and hollering like something out of a bad cartoon.

Carter assumed Kaylee was as annoyed by the distraction as he was. "Can you believe that?" He rolled his eyes, and she grew more irritated. "That kid is way too old to act like that, and you'd think his mom would've figured out how to discipline him by now. Good grief."

Instead of agreeing, she glared at him. "You really are a jackass." She picked up Valentino, made sure his leash was still securely attached to his harness, and handed him to Carter. "If you can watch him for a minute, I'd like to go help my friend, who happens to be one of the best moms I know. Her son is a sweet little boy. He's autistic, *not* a brat. My nephew is in his class at school, one of his best friends. Just shut up with your judgmental observations, I'll be right back."

Carter took the pooch and watched as Kaylee rushed over to the woman in distress. The mom hugged her and bent down to talk to her son as Kaylee said something to the woman who had meant well, but had pushed the kid into a full out tantrum when she'd touched him. The woman nodded and walked away. From his seat, he could see and hear most of what went on.

Kaylee spoke to the child as if everything was going like normal. "Hey, Seth, I like those sneakers. Are they new?" How she ignored all that screaming and kicking, he didn't know. "Have you shown 'em to Nick yet? Bet he'll want to get a pair just like that."

The kid's yells calmed for a brief second, but then he went right back at it. She whispered something to the mom, then darted off to the pizza booth. She came back with a big slice of pepperoni pizza and plenty of napkins.

"Seth, look what I've got for you. Pepperoni is Nick's favorite, so I hope you like it." The boy paused his fit and gazed at the ceiling. His mother looked like she was about to cry in relief. Both women ignored a few ignorant comments from people in the food court. "Come on, there's a table over there under the skylight where you and your mom can sit."

Miraculously, the kid quietened down and stood up. He looked toward the floor and flapped his hands, but he followed her.

After she set the pizza on the table and scooted the chair out for him, she stood back to give him plenty of space to take his seat. "Is it okay if I sit with you, across the table, while your mom gets some food? I think she's pretty hungry."

Seth gave a half nod, so Kaylee kept talking to him about pizza and toy cars while his mom hurried to buy some tacos. When Seth's mom returned, Kaylee said goodbye to them both.

Her smile turned into a frown as she approached Carter.

"That was incredible. How did you know what to do?" Carter was in awe of the way she'd handled the situation. His own temper would've kicked in after all the initial racket the kid had made.

"I have a heart. Seth and my nephew buddied up at school since they're both obsessed with Hot Wheels." Kaylee took Valentino and the tote bag, and then pushed the chair she'd sat in earlier up to the table. "Nick makes sure none of the other kids say mean things to his friend. Too bad you don't share the same compassion." She turned to walk away.

"Wait, I thought we were going to get something to eat." Carter stood up and reached for her arm. She pulled away.

"Don't even think about it. I've gotta go."

Valentino pointed a look of confusion from one of them to the other. Kaylee headed off in the direction that would take her the furthest from Carter.

"Wait, where do you want to meet when it's my turn to take Valentino in a few days? We haven't even discussed that yet." Carter tried to follow her, but she was hell-bent on ignoring him.

"Text me or something. If you can come down off your high horse long enough."

With that, she was gone. With impressive speed, she zigzagged around shoppers and mall rats and was out of his line of vision in seconds.

When would he learn to stop offending her?

Chapter Seven

Four days later, Kaylee walked into the bar where Carter lived and worked. She'd dreaded seeing him again, but she dreaded handing Valentino over to him even more.

Carter had called a couple days after the mall incident to make plans for the next exchange. He'd also asked to borrow the baby gate she'd mentioned using to keep Valentino confined to parts of her house when she was in the shower or ran to the mailbox. He said he worried that the dog might get out from behind the bar and get lost. For some reason, she got the distinct impression that his fear of things that might happen, already had. Hence her skyrocketing anxiety.

She carried Valentino tucked under her arm like a clutch purse. At less than four pounds, she could barely feel his weight as she maneuvered the cumbersome baby gate around the tables. She'd bought it to corral her niece and nephew when they were toddlers. Five- and eight-year-old Natalee and Nick had outgrown the gate and were happy to pass it along to Valentino.

It was three on the dot, she saw from a glance at her watch, but Carter was nowhere to be seen. She asked the man behind the bar, and after he petted the Yorkie's head and gave him a scratch behind the ear, he asked her to have a seat and said his boss should be back any minute.

She and Valentino waited in a booth beside the windows for fifteen agonizing minutes. Apparently the jerk had no qualms about wasting more of her time. The afternoon bartender must have felt bad about her wait since he brought her a ginger ale and a bowl of pretzels, on the house, with a side of Valentino's bacon flavored treats shaped like little piggies.

Finally, a flashy red sports car pulled into the parking lot and steered around to the side of the building. Too bad he hadn't stood her and Valentino up entirely, but, of course, she wasn't lucky enough to avoid having to see him. He wanted his turn with the dog.

She heard throaty laughter coming from the back of the building. He must have come through the other door. Kaylee checked her watch once more, and it was nearly three thirty. She didn't have any other place she had to be, but she hated to let a late inconsiderate person waste her afternoon.

Carter sauntered in through the door by the bar, his most charming grin turned up full strength. Good for him, not beating himself up for being so tardy.

Valentino saw him and barked. He turned in a circle and hopped up on the table, his little tail wagging a mile a minute. She couldn't help but smile at the sweet little love bug, and turned to see if Carter was watching.

Nope, he sure wasn't. His eyes were trained on the busty blonde chick beside him. At first, Kaylee thought it was the shorter floozy from the coffee shop the day she and Carter had first met and fell head over heels in dislike. But no, a second glance proved she'd never seen this woman before.

Whoever it was touched his arm and they both laughed over what she'd said to him. Kaylee shook her head in disgust as they finally headed over to the table. They all exchanged quick hellos as Carter slid into his side of the booth after Blondie, who was holding a shopping bag and giggling like a fruitcake. His date reached out to grab Valentino off the table, but he ducked away and ran across the table to play with his buddy, Carter.

Kaylee bit her tongue, literally. The salt from the pretzels she'd eaten made it sting. Her first impulse had been to let him have it for making her wait so long, again, while he was out gallivanting around with . . . *that.* She decided against it, reluctantly, since it seemed to bother Valentino when they argued.

"So glad you could make it." Kaylee left it at that, and pointed an exaggerated glance at her watch.

"We're late, sorry, that's my bad entirely." Blondie uttered a loud giggle that sounded like machine gun fire. "Carter took me to lunch, and when he told me about the puppy, I just had to stop by the pet store. Look what we got for it." She dug around in the bag and pulled out a toy rubber chicken. "Hey dog, look at the toy we got for you!" She squeaked it in his face and beamed an idiot's grin.

If it were possible for a Yorkie's nose

to turn up, Valentino's would have. His brown eyes darted from the idiot to the ugly chicken-shaped plastic thing being thrust in his face. The earsplitting EEE-EEE coming from the noisemaker in the toy's butt seemed to really tick him off. He growled at it and backed away.

"Oh, so cute, he's saying how much he wikes his wittle toy!" The genius kept on squeaking it.

Kaylee bit her tongue again to keep from telling this raving she-moron exactly what Valentino had on his mind. Regardless of how cute his growls might sound, it was easy to see that he was upset.

Valentino started barking, a little fear creeping into his eyes as Blondie thrust the thing even closer to his face. He backed up again. His foot met with the end of the table, and then thin air.

Carter caught him. His jaw clenched, and he shifted the dog to the elbow farthest away from the mad squeaker.

Kaylee blared her eyes at him. When he said nothing, she couldn't help it. As nicely as she could, she told Blondie, "Nice of you to buy him a toy, but he's so little, we have to remember he can't jump off furniture, or anything dangerous like that." She couldn't address her by name since Carter hadn't bothered to introduce them.

"Oh, I know," Blondie said in whiny baby talk, "he's so wittle bitty. It's okay, his daddy caught him."

This chick exemplified those cheesy dumb blonde jokes Kaylee had hated her entire life, since they shared the same hair color.

She thought she saw Carter wince. How could he stand to date this woman?

"Hey! Let's try on his other stuff!" She dumped the rest of the contents of the shopping bag on the table, and then, as if it were the most natural thing in the world to her, she leaned over and gave Carter a big kiss on the cheek. Just like a toddler, she added a loud 'Mmmm-waa' at the end, and then she tried to kiss Valentino. At least he managed to wiggle away from those over-glossed red lips.

"Where is the ladies room?" Kaylee felt sick. She didn't know why seeing Carter with one of his bimbos would upset her to the point of nausea, but it had. If she didn't walk it off, splash a little cold water on her face, she was either going to puke or explode.

She trudged off in the direction he pointed in. It took her a good five minutes to calm down after she finally chalked her feelings up to worry and anxiety over leaving Valentino with Carter and his stupid girlfriend. And she wasn't looking forward to spending a lonely evening without the pooch to keep her company. Maybe she could pick up a bottle of wine and rent a romantic comedy from Redbox on her way home. That put her in a better mood as she returned to the table. As soon as her butt hit the booth cushion, however, her attitude changed.

"Please, can I take the puppy wuppie for a walk?" Blondie whined.

Carter held the dog, but Valentino leaned back as far away from the woman as he could. It was obvious the dog didn't like her. He sure had better taste than the person who held him.

"It wants to show off the new leash I bought it. Don't you, boy?" She leaned over, too close the dog's face. The Yorkie kicked and squirmed, barking for her to give him some space.

Why wasn't Carter telling her to put a sock in it and leave the poor dog alone? Even he couldn't be too stupid to see that Valentino wanted no part of entertaining the other idiot.

Carter hesitated, then said to Kaylee, "Could you take him for a minute, see if you can calm him down?" Carter set the dog back down on the table when she nodded, and Valentino couldn't get to her fast enough. The leash trailed behind him.

He stopped in front of Kaylee and nuzzled noses with her as she petted him. Then Valentino yelped. Kaylee stared down into his eyes. He was shaking and whining in distress.

Blondie had picked up the leash and tried to pull the dog toward her. Rude, yes, but Kaylee didn't understand why that made Valentino yelp.

Kaylee picked him up to see if his fur was tangled in his harness, which had happened before. But the harness she'd put on him earlier wasn't on him now. "What—"

Then she saw the collar. A tacky blue fake leather piece of crap with gaudy rhinestones.

"Carter, what the heck is this? You know he can't wear a collar." She unbuckled it and threw it across the table. "What's wrong with you? Give me back his harness."

"I gave it to him. There's nothing

wrong with that collar." Blondie huffed. "Carter, put that back on him. Right now."

"Over my dead body!" Kaylee couldn't help but lose her temper. "This is not your dog and, quite frankly, none of our business. Just so you know, Yorkshire terriers, especially teacups, aren't supposed to wear collars. Anything on his throat, like a collar or heaven forbid, a choke chain, could damage his trachea. That's why he always wears a harness."

"Well, he's not your dog either and I don't give a crap what you think." Blondie put her hand on Carter's arm. "Put it back on him."

Kaylee opened and closed her mouth, trying not to blurt something she shouldn't as she hugged Valentino to her chest. Valentino licked Kaylee's cheek, then seemed to shoot a look at the blonde idiot.

"No, Dora." Carter's voice was firm. "Not if it's going to hurt him. Sorry. I know I must've read that the other day, but I forgot it. I was more focused on memorizing the foods he couldn't eat. Is he okay?"

"Oh, he's fine." The blonde twirled an over-dyed strand of hair around her finger. "I'm sure the collar didn't hurt it, no matter what she thinks."

"First, Valentino is a him, not an it." Carter's voice was stoic, but Kaylee sensed anger just beneath the surface despite how calm he appeared to be. "Secondly, for the moment, Valentino is as much Kaylee's as he is mine. We both want what's best for him. And third, no way are we putting any collar back on him, because she's right. I apologize to all three of you for forgetting, you, little guy, most of all." He reached across the table to scratch behind Valentino's little Yorkie ears.

"Fine, put that cheap red thingie back on him, for all I care." Dora, aka Blondie, rolled her eyes and picked at her fingernails. "I gotta run, anyways."

"The red harness is Corinthian leather and made in Italy." Kaylee grabbed the harness from Carter and put it back on Valentino, who was still shaking from the incident. "Pamela bought it on a business trip to Rome last year. I'm pretty sure it cost more than the five dollars you laid out for that sparkly piece of crap. But whatever."

"Come on, I'll walk you out." Carter stood so Dora could slide out of the booth. "Excuse me, Kaylee. I'll be right back."

Kaylee didn't bother to respond since he was already striding toward the back exit. They had driven up in Carter's silly red car, so Dora must have come earlier. Or the night before. Kaylee's heart sank.

Unlike earlier, Carter didn't keep her waiting this time. He was back after a couple of minutes and returned to the booth.

"Sorry about that." He looked

straight at her, and she thought his eyes were sincere. "Honestly, I wasn't even paying attention to what she picked out at the store, but I should have remembered the no-no list when she put the collar on him."

He probably hadn't noticed because he was too busy flirting with Dora. A thought crossed her mind that made her queasy again.

"I brought the baby gate you asked to borrow." Kaylee drew in a deep breath and put her hands on the table. Valentino had just walked across the table to Carter and was sniffing his shirt, probably trying not to gag if Dora's cheap perfume had rubbed off on it. "Look, mistakes happen, I understand that. And I don't mean this the wrong way, but are you sure it wouldn't be easier for you to let Valentino come back home with me? Who you run around with is your business, but I'm afraid Valentino will be neglected if Dora sleeps over. And for heaven's sake, please promise me you won't leave him alone with her? In the short time she was here, she nearly made him topple off the table before she tried to choke him to death with that crappy collar of hers."

"No, I don't want you to take him back with you, but I can understand why you're upset." Carter looked a bit sheepish. "I'm really not as incompetent as you think."

"Between nearly killing him with chocolate ice cream and letting your girlfriend pretend he's a dress up doll, what else am I supposed to think?"

"Wait." He held his hands up, palms facing her. "She is *not* my girlfriend."

"Okay. Your booty call then. Whatever."

"Dora's not that either. At least not mine." Carter shook his head. "She's a regular here at the bar. I didn't take her out to lunch. She came in Quizno's while I was eating a meatball sub, sat down at my table. When I told her I had to come back here to get Valentino, she insisted I let her buy him a gift. She was only trying to be nice."

"Yeah, then how's she getting home, or wherever she's headed for?" Kaylee realized she didn't have a right to ask. If he was lying about her sleeping over, or whatever they did together, gross, it was none of her business. As long as it didn't affect the dog in their joint care.

His piercing blue eyes danced above his twisted grin. "Why are you so concerned about my love life all of a sudden?"

"I'm not. If you two rode in your car, I'm just wondering how she'd get home unless her car was already parked here. Not that I care, I just don't like being lied to."

"Jealous much?"

"Heck no!"

"We pulled up in separate cars, Miss Know-it-all." She didn't like the way he grinned at her, and she did hate to be wrong. Especially when she'd been so smug about it. "She parked near my spot in the back and we walked in together. Next time, should we call you before we walk into the bar, where I live?"

"Sorry." She hadn't actually seen the woman in the car, so now she felt like a pea brain. It was none of her business, like she'd said before. "It wasn't cool to call you a liar." She grinned at him, hoping to lighten the situation. "A little incompetent, yep, I can prove that, but at least you're honest."

They discussed where the next exchange would be, and after Carter had sworn on his life that he'd never in a million years leave Valentino in Dora's care, ever, Kaylee said she needed to go. Carter and Valentino walked her to the car on their way around the block before his shift started.

"Please don't forget to bring the gate when you drop Valentino off."

"Sure thing." He held her car door open, ever the gentleman.

He was holding the dog, so she leaned in to kiss the pooch on his head. "See you soon, love bug."

When she straightened up, her face was in Carter's personal space. His eyes were even more gorgeous close up. She startled when she realized she was staring at the man, but he seemed to stare back with the same intensity.

"Well, see you soon too, I guess."

Valentino wiggled, kicking his legs in a comical way as he lunged for Kaylee. He didn't want to see her go.

They both reached for the dog to keep him from falling.

"Watch it there, little guy." Carter stood so close, both of them supporting the dog, that she could feel his body heat.

Kaylee fidgeted for her keys.

"Yeah, see you later." Carter leaned in and kissed her. He pulled her toward him, careful not to squash the Yorkie between them.

Kaylee kissed him back. This was

the last thing she'd ever expected, so what had gotten into him? Or into her?

She pulled away and jumped into her car so she wouldn't have to look at him. "Bye," she said, and she was out of there.

Chapter Eight

Kaylee paced the length of the Flicker and Flame as she waited for Carter to arrive with Valentino. She'd spent more time on her hair and makeup than usual, and even dressed up a little, in a flowery skirt and lavender V-neck sweater. Ben had whistled and pretended not to know who she was when he came in, since she usually pittered around the shop in jeans and boots instead of skirts and heels.

She still wasn't sure how she felt about Carter. That kiss. If they'd been drinking or something before it happened, it would've made more sense,

but they'd had a blowout, with his being late and the whole Dora incident.
Nothing there screamed 'it's time for a
kiss.' But he had and she'd returned it.

Awkward.

Carter texted the day after the kiss,
to see how Valentino was doing. They'd
exchanged a few messages back and
forth each day since then, and she got
the vibe that he might ask her out. She
was conflicted about how to deal with
it if he did. Carter Hartley was exactly
the kind of man she wanted to avoid.
After she'd caught her ex-fiancé messing around with her friend, she certainly didn't want another playboy in her
personal life. But Carter, with all his
faults—womanizing, jumping to judg-
ments about people, being reckless and
irresponsible—was a gentleman. His
manners clashed with every other
opinion she had of him. Valentino
loved him, and since the dog wouldn't
bow down to letting some people even
pet him, that meant something to her.

Honestly, he seemed as happy to see Carter as he did to see her.

At least he got there on time. She'd given him the address but hadn't mentioned that it was her shop. His car pulled in right on schedule, but he took his time getting out and walking inside.

"Hi there." Way to sound like a simpering idiot, she chided herself. She tried to pretend her enthusiasm was focused on the dog. "Hey, Valentino, my little love bug, you happy to see me?" He squirmed toward her and wagged his tail when she patted him, but Carter didn't hand him over.

"He's all right." Carter seemed more reserved than usual, and he wasn't looking in her eyes. "But, I have to show you something. Don't freak out, okay."

"What did you do?"

"Nothing." She saw Carter swallow hard, like he was nervous. "I know he has an appointment with the groomers

119

later this afternoon, right?"

"Yes, but what are you trying so hard not to tell me? Is he alright? Tell me you did not let that Dora person put a collar on him. I swear, if he's hurt—"

"Haven't seen her, and he's not hurt." Carter took off Valentino's harness and adjusted the dog's sweater. "Don't freak out, but he's got a major hair don't going on." He pulled the sweater up to show Kaylee.

"OMG, you've got to be kidding me!" A wad of gum was matted in the Yorkie's fur. "So much of his pretty hair is stuck in a ball off Bubble Yum! I can't believe you. Pamela would totally freak out if she saw him like this." Pamela did not like the look of short puppy cuts on Yorkshire terriers, so Valentino's hair was kept mid-length for the breed while still shorter than what you'd see in the show ring.

"Lucky for us that she's not here." Carter did seem upset about the situation.

"How did this happen? And how long has he been like this." Kaylee took a closer look and twitched her nose. "What is that smell?"

"One of the customers threw their gum at the trash can behind the bar last night. I don't know if it hit Valentino or if he laid on it after it landed on the floor. Doesn't matter. It's a mess either way."

"Why is the gum slimy?" She poked it with her finger. "Gum is not supposed to be slimy." She looked at him and waited for an explanation.

"That would be the peanut butter."

She glared at him like he was a lunatic.

"A couple of customers tried to help get the gum out of his hair, but it was already stuck like that. Some guy said his wife used peanut butter to get gum out of his daughter's hair when she fell asleep with it in her mouth and woke up stuck to the pillowcase."

"That was a fantastic idea, huh?"

"I'm sorry, but it was the best I could come up with at the time." Carter shook his head. "It's not like I did this to him on purpose."

"I know." Kaylee took a closer look, tried to see underneath the wad, but it was a mess. "He's going to need a major haircut to get that out. I'll probably have to leave here earlier and call ahead to let the groomer know about the gum. They'll have a hard time cutting it out before they even think about how to style his 'do so it doesn't look ridiculous." It really wasn't Carter's fault, so she didn't want to make him feel any worse about it than he already did. "Good thing there's nothing important going on here this afternoon, so I can leave early."

"Your boss should be glad he won't have to pay you overtime." Carter looked around the shop and laughed. "Who buys enough candles to keep this place in business, anyway? Hasn't been a single person in here since I walked in." He lowered his voice to ask, "Is that guy who went in the back the owner? Man, I feel sorry for him."

"No." Kaylee felt her ears burning. She was afraid she was going to cry. "Ben's my employee."

"Oh, so you're the manager. Cool, I didn't know we had that in common." He scanned the place again. He picked up a random candle and snickered. "You might want to find a better place to work, before this joint closes down." He glanced at the candle in his hand again. "I mean, come on. Twilight raspberry." He picked up another. "Lemon Dazzle. These are the dumbest names for candles I've ever heard. Sound more like bad cocktails."

Kaylee's heart broke. Didn't he care that she put her heart and soul into running this business? That coming to work was the only thing that kept her going when everything else in her life fell apart? "Not the manager. I'm the owner." She sniffed hard, then pinched herself on the arm to hold back her tears.

"Oh." Carter set the candles back down on the display table. "Sorry, I didn't know." He was quiet for a full minute.

Kaylee stared at him, at a total loss for words. It wasn't often that someone destroyed her world and wounded her pride with a few offhanded comments.

"The building will most likely appreciate in value when that new subdivision gets finished down the street," he said.

"I own the business, you jackass, not the building."

Her first instincts about Carter had been right after all. A self-centered jerk. She had no inclination to spend one more second in his presence. To think she'd seriously considered going out with him! The sooner he left her shop, the better. And on top of her hurt feelings, she had to deal with getting the gum out of Valentino's hair while making sure the groomer didn't give him a buzz cut.

"Will you please bring in the gate you borrowed?" He hadn't come in with anything except Valentino. "I'd like to go on to the groomers."

"I knew I was forgetting something." Carter took a step toward her, his palms up in apology. "I'm so sorry. I would never have said those things if I knew . . . . Hey, this candle shop is kind of nice, now that I think about it. Owning the bar one day is my dream, so I totally know how much work you must have put in to establish this."

"Yeah, well, just get the gate." Kaylee was in no mood to listen to a load of bull crap just then.

"It's still at my place. With the whole gum thing stressing me out, I com-pletely forgot about it. Tell you what. I can bring it by tonight." He flashed a charming grin he probably practiced in front of the mirror. "I'll take you out to

125

dinner to make up for, well, everything I've done wrong since we met."

"No thanks." Kaylee walked to the door and held it open for him. "I'll see if my sister has one I can borrow."

"If you don't want to go out with me tonight, Valentine's Day is Sunday. I'd really like to—"

"Bye Carter." She jerked her head toward the open door to speed up his departure. "I've got to go."

"Sorry to bother you, Pamela," Kaylee said into her cell. With Valentino getting a bubble gum makeover from the groomer, she thought this would be the best time to make the call. She hoped this would put an end to all the stress she'd had to deal with the past few weeks. "But I really need to talk to you about something important."

She spilled everything that was on her mind and emphasized that the haircut her Yorkie was about to get was in no way, shape, or form her fault. She told Pamela that with the gum problem on top of the incident with the chocolate, and after that bimbo had nearly choked him with her bedazzled collar, she was worried sick. "I'm afraid Valentino isn't getting enough supervision at Carter's bar."

She waited for Pamela to say something.

"Is that all you need to tell me?" Pamela sounded bored, not at all concerned. "Anything else?"

"Like I said, I'm worried sick when Valentino is with Carter. I would truly appreciate it if Valentino could go ahead and come live with me."

Silence on the other end.

"So, what do you think?"

"I simply don't have time to deal with this childish drama between you two." Pamela sighed into the receiver. Why wasn't she more concerned about the welfare of her beloved Yorkshire terrier than having to take one urgent phone call? "Carter called weeks ago to complain about you nagging him over silly things like ice cream and coffee. I have no idea what he was talking about. Now you call to bother me about chewing gum and some ditsy girlfriend of his. Really, this is ridiculous."

"I'm sorry. Didn't mean to upset you, but I'm—"

"Look, if you two can't last out the month to see who should get Valentino, I'll have no other choice but to euthanize the dog." Pamela added sarcastically, "Would that make things easier for you?"

Chapter Nine

Kaylee called Carter right after she hung up with Pamela. He was now the second to last person in the world she wanted to speak to, but given the circumstances, she had to communicate with him. She paced in front of the groomer's place since Valentino was still inside getting bubble gum cut out of his fur.

"Look, we have a huge problem. Please, just hear me out."

"I would never hang up on you. What's wrong?" Concern resonated through his deep voice. "You alright? Val okay?"

"For now. Don't worry, he's still getting your gum trimmed out of his hair." Kaylee took a deep breath to calm down. She was both furious and heartsick over what Pamela said she might do. She'd had to stop her tears before she'd dialed the phone and did not want to sound like a hysterical female. "You are not going to believe what Fairbanks just said."

She told him about the conversation verbatim. Carter was outraged, and called Pamela a name that fit her a heck of a lot better than Pammy.

"Whether you hate me or not, please, we have to work together on this, to keep Valentino safe." Kaylee heard her voice shake uncontrollably, then the sniffles came that she couldn't silence.

"Kaylee, I don't hate you, but even if I did, you know how much I love that dog." Carter sounded very shaken up himself. "There's nothing to worry about if neither of us complains to her again. As a matter of fact, we should both make a point of not speaking to her until the end of the month, after a decision is made."

"But what if—"

"No, don't go there." Carter's voice was soothing. It felt like a safe haven, like a velvet blanket she'd like to wrap herself up in. "I promise I won't let that happen. No matter what."

"Thank you. I'm glad I called instead of texting." The door opened and the groomer waved to get her attention. The woman held Valentino, who, thankfully, still looked like a frou-frou little pampered Yorkie instead of a shaved mouse. "Hey, I gotta go. Valentino's all done.

"Look," Carter said, "why don't you go out with me. We can call an official truce, and I swear I'll do everything in my power to keep my foot out of my big mouth. It's Valentine's Day this Sunday and I know this cozy little place downtown—"

"Sorry." Too many feelings coursed

through her just then to make a sane decision. She obviously had terrible taste in men, and she was still afraid Carter shared too many of the same traits with her last boyfriend. "I already have plans for Valentine's Day."

Carter was silent. Her intention wasn't to hurt his feelings, but in light of all the things he'd said about her candle shop, she wouldn't lose sleep over it if she had. But she did intend to get along with him and was glad he also put Valentino's needs in front of his own, especially after what Pamela said.

Kaylee wasn't lying, but she sure as heck wasn't about to let him know her plans were to entertain her niece and nephew while her sister had a romantic dinner date with her hubby.

"Oh. Alright then." Disappointment played heavily in his voice, but then he cleared his throat. "Call me if you need me. To talk about Val, or whatever."

A hailstorm of emotions forbid Kaylee from even thinking about the hopeful tone in his voice, about the way she'd spent the last four days thinking about how she would say yes if he asked her out. Or, on the other hand, about the way he'd run her business acumen into the ground an hour ago.

"Okay, thanks. Bye."

That evening she had a delicious spaghetti and meatball dinner with her sister, Kendra, and her family. She took Valentino, and after a five-minute lecture on everything her niece and nephew were not allowed to do to him or with him, the kids had an absolute ball playing with the little love bug. Kendra even cut up a special meatball and let Natalee feed him in her lap at super, with a fork.

They stuffed plates into the dishwasher and tucked the kiddos in after a bedtime story from Auntie Kaylee. Kendra's husband, Alex, snuck away to his man cave in the basement, since he'd begged off having to sit between them while they drank vino and cried over some sappy romantic comedy. Despite Natalee pleading with her mom for the dog to sleep with her, Valentino sat between the sisters on the couch, curled up and snuggled into a fluffy throw pillow.

"Tell you what," Kendra said as she fiddled with the remote. "We'll save the movie until after E! News goes off. And while we watch, you tell me what's going on between you and this other dog walker who's in the running to be Valentino's doggie daddy."

Kaylee poured wine for them both. She'd already told her about the ultimatum Pamela dropped that afternoon. Kendra had taken one look at her sister when she'd gotten there and told her to spill it. Good thing, since Kaylee had actually relaxed over dinner and couldn't even bear to think about what that horrible woman had threatened to do to the poor little Yorkie.

"Not much to tell. Other than us both being willing to do whatever it takes to keep Valentino safe, we really don't get along very well."

"You sure? You always sound kind of flustered when you talk about this guy. Carlson, is it?"

"Carter," Kaylee corrected her.

"Looks like even saying his name makes you smile." Kendra took a sip of wine. "So tell me what you think is wrong with him."

"He's just not my type. An arrogant, judgmental ladies man." Kaylee ran her finger around the rim of the wine glass. "But he really does care about Valentino, doesn't he, boy?" She scratched the dog behind his pointy ears.

"It wouldn't kill you to let your guard down, you know." Kendra gave her a look. "Every guy you meet isn't going to break your heart the way that creep

Evan did. You *are* over him, right?"

"Over and done with him long ago." Kaylee took a big sip of wine. "Mindy too."

"I never did like that girl. Too stuck on herself." Kendra saw Kaylee flinch. "Sleeping with Evan behind your back was low, even for her."

"Yeah, but you can see why the whole deal gave me trust issues, right?" Kaylee picked Valentino up off the pillow and snuggled him against her chest. "When two of the people I trusted most in this world screw me over, it's not real easy to open up to a new guy who's likely to do the same thing. Or worse." She swigged more vino. "Actually, what could be worse? Tell me and make me feel like less of a loser."

"Duh, worse would've been marrying the S.O.B. and finding out he was messing with Mindy after you'd had a few kids with him. You're lucky you caught them when you did." Kendra leaned over and thumped her sister on the forehead. Valentino growled a little, which made them both laugh. "Enough wasted breath on those two. Tell me why you won't go out with this Carter person."

"If he'd asked me before he insulted my shop, I would've gone out with him. But that just proved how judgmental he is. He's always late, not to mention the women I've seen him hanging out with are beyond sleazy." Kaylee straightened Valentino's hair bow. "And he's just so conceited."

"Yeah?" Kendra grinned behind her wine glass. "What makes him think he's so hot?"

"His piercing blue eyes, his head full of dark curly hair, that smile, and he probably works out all the time since he's built like a gladiator." Kaylee rolled her eyes and tried not to think about Carter's physique.

"Sounds terrible." Kendra's sarcasm hit home. "Why don't you give the man

137

a chance? Go out with him a time or two, what do you have to lose?"

"Um, my dignity."

"Just think about it. You have little Valentino here in common. How bad could the guy be?"

Chapter Ten

Two days later, Kaylee cut into a pan of special dairy-free homemade double-chocolate brownies she'd made for her niece. Natalee was bummed out because she couldn't eat all the yummy chocolate heart-shaped candy and cupcakes like the other kids in her kindergarten class. Kaylee knew her pain, since they shared the joy of being lactose intolerant. That Kaylee's sister and Natalee's brother could both digest ice cream and milkshakes without rolling on the floor with agonizing stomach cramps was just ridiculously unfair.

She always tried to go all out to help her sister make sure Natalee didn't miss out on anything sentimental or gooey because of it. She filled a red heart-shaped box full of perfectly cut square brownies she'd dusted with red sugar when they came out of the oven. 'Be Mine' was written in glittery red letters on the white ribbon glued to the lid. Her niece was going to love it. She put the lid on and set it on the kitchen table beside the box of Valentine candy with a race car on the front she'd picked up for Nick.

Her dining table sat a bit high, so to keep Natalee from having to struggle to get into the chair later, Kaylee moved her retro stool in place at the head of the table. It had steps that pulled out so the five-year-old could easily climb up and take a seat.

Lucky for Kaylee and her empty stomach that a couple brownies crumbled and didn't look pretty enough to make it into the box. Not to let them go to waste, she taste tested them with a glass of almond milk. De-freakin'-licious.

Her sister was supposed to bring the kids over later that afternoon, so she had time to take a shower and catch a cheesy Valentine special on Lifetime before they would get there.

"Come on, boy." Valentino trotted beside her to the bedroom. Her heart ached every time she thought about the cruel thing Pamela threatened to do if she and Carter couldn't suck it up until a decision was made about where the Yorkie would live. What Kaylee had mistaken as Pamela's devotion to the dog had merely been Pamela's latest pet project, so to speak. She apparently cared more about setting up her new office than making sure that sweet little pooch lived a long, happy life in a wonderful home.

Before she hit the shower, she picked Valentino up and set him on the pillow he liked to sleep on. "Take a nap before those kids get here, Valentino, because I'm sure they're going to chase you down and play fetch until you can't stand it."

He was still resting there when she cracked opened the bathroom door to check on him before she used the blow drier. Valentino raised his head and barked when he saw what was in her hand. She had to dry her hair with the door closed because the racket it made drove the dog nuts. Probably more flashbacks from his commercial days.

She got dressed and dabbed on a little makeup, in case any long-pining secret admirer like the one in the movie she'd just watched should happen to show up to whisk her away to some island paradise with a dozen roses and an engagement ring.

"Don't bet on that happening," she said to Valentino when she walked back into her bedroom. But he wasn't on the bed. "Hey, boy, where did you go this time?" Not under the bed, or in the closet. He was so tiny, the little scamp could hide almost anywhere.

On her way to the living room to look for him, she froze. From the hall, she could see her kitchen table.

"No!"

Valentino stood on the table. The heart-shaped lid was on the floor. He looked up at her, licked his lips, and then ducked his head for another mouthful of double-chocolate brownie.

Chapter Eleven

Kaylee sat in the waiting room when Carter rushed in. She ran to meet him, crying harder when he hugged her.

"How's he doing?" Carter combed his fingers through his unruly dark curls. "What did the vet say?"

"She'll be back out in a minute." Kaylee blew her nose and took a deep breath. "The peroxide she told me to give him made him throw up, which should help. She's running some blood tests now, and doing an ECG." It killed her to know Valentino was suffering because she was too stupid to make sure he didn't get into the brownies.

She would never be able to live with herself if he didn't pull through.

"Thanks for calling me." Carter sounded sincere. "Especially after the stuff I said the last time I saw you."

She'd called him as she drove to the veterinary clinic, and texted her sister to tell her what was happening. She had to give Nick and Natalee a rain check on their Valentine gifts, since they had to spend the night with their grandparents now instead of at her house.

"I had to let you know what was going on. You are the only person who loves that dog as much as I do. I'm so sorry." Kaylee sobbed even harder. "I read you the riot act about being irresponsible and look what I did. If he doesn't make it, it'll be all my fault."

Carter hugged her again, let her soak his sweater with tears as he held her. "No Kaylee, it's not your fault."

"Don't argue with her," said someone behind Kaylee. She pulled away from his warm embrace only to see Dora leaning on the door jamb, smirking at her. "You fussed at me over a collar, and then you go and poison the poor dog. You should be ashamed of yourself. Too lazy to move that chocolate out of Carter's dog's reach."

"I'm sorry!"

"Get out of here." Carter's voice boomed through the waiting room of the emergency veterinary clinic.

Kaylee's heart broke. Carter had every right to hate her, she knew that, but she couldn't leave until she knew if Valentino would pull through. She looked up to apologize to him again, to beg him not to make her go.

He was marching across the room at full speed. He pushed open the door and pointed outside.

"I appreciate the ride since my car's getting detailed, but get out. Don't you ever speak to her like that again."

"Fine. You two nut jobs deserve each other, getting all worked up over a stupid dog." Dora stepped one foot outside, then said, "I should find a better place to hang out since you care more about that dumb dog than your customers."

"Don't ever set foot in my bar again. I mean it." He slammed the door in her face.

The veterinarian walked out before Kaylee had a chance to thank him for getting rid of her.

"He'll have to stay overnight. He's got a good chance of pulling through, since you found him while he was eating the brownies and rushed him right over." Dr. Davenport spoke in a caring voice, but she didn't gloss over the fact that Valentino might not make it through the night. "Since he's so small, it wouldn't take very much chocolate to give him a fatal dose of theobromine. But he's on an IV for fluids and we're giving him activated charcoal to help flush it out of his system. We'll just have to see how the next few hours go."

Apprentice veterinarians stayed through the late shift to keep an eye on all the patients. They would call Dr. Davenport if an emergency arose or another pet was brought in.

"This whole thing was my fault, not yours," Carter said. "If I had brought the gate back to you like I was supposed to, Valentino wouldn't have got to the chocolate brownies. This is on me." He shook his head and looked down, then reached out to pet Valentino's side. "We're all he's got. I'm still mad that Pamela turned out to be so cold and heartless. Seriously, how could someone just threaten to, you know, hurt an innocent dog like Val?" He couldn't even say the words out loud, that Pam had threatened to euthanize the dog. "She'd better not ask for one more favor in the bar. As a matter of fact, I don't plan to ever speak to her again."

She noticed that he wasn't calling her Pammy anymore, something that would have made her very happy, if not for the dire situation.

Kaylee and Carter sat beside Valentino's crate all night, the wire door open, one of them constantly holding his paw or stroking his head. They had ample opportunity to really get to know each other as they made small talk to help pass the time.

At three in the morning, Valentino started to twitch uncontrollably. Kaylee picked him up and cradled him against her chest, scared to death that he was dying. Carter ran to get help. The vet in training quickly administered a shot and then checked his vitals.

"He's had a seizure, but I think he's going to be okay. That can happen with theobromine. Holler if it happens again, but it probably won't." He patted them both on their arms and went to attend to a diabetic cat down the hall.

They prayed Valentino would wake up in the morning.

Chapter Twelve

Pamela Fairbanks sent her assistant to the candle shop to meet with Kaylee and Carter on March first. In the end, Pamela had decided to let Valentino live permanently with Kaylee, mainly because she had a fenced in backyard the Yorkie liked to run and play in, a much safer environment than the crowded bar. The dog's registration papers were signed over to Kaylee but Carter wasn't saying goodbye to Valentino anytime soon. He had the freedom to visit with the dog any time he wanted, as often as he liked.

He and Kaylee had gone on their

first date after Valentino recovered. They entrusted him to Kendra's care while they went out for dinner and a movie, and that date had left them both hopelessly smitten with each other.

After the last paper was signed and the ordeal of Valentino's forever home was forever solved, Ruthie ran her hand over the pooch's right side. Then she nearly doubled over laughing.

"Pam would have a full out fit if she could see this hairdo." Ruthie touched the bald spot on the dog's side where the groomer had cut out the bubble gum. Like Kaylee had asked, the groomers had tried to hide the place as best they could without making him look ridiculous.

Then Ruthie held up Valentino's paw and ran her thumb over the shaved spot on his leg where the IV had been.

"Yeah, but from the left, he still looks perfect." Kaylee laughed when Ruthie joked about clipping his hair back with a few barrettes to camouflage it. "I'll get it evened up when it grows out a little more.

"Well, one thing about it, I'm glad this little dog has a loving new home," Ruthie said. "And it looks like he's pretty good at playing matchmaker. The three of you look great together."

"That was the best Valentine gift I've ever got." Carter meant it with all his heart. "When we knew Valentino was going to make it, Kaylee let me kiss her to celebrate." Carter gave her a quick peck on the lips and thought he tasted strawberry ChapStick. He kissed her again to confirm it. "I'm a lucky man."

They told Ruthie goodbye and walked down the sidewalk to Carter's car.

Kaylee snapped Valentino into his car seat before they drove off into the sunset, hand in hand, with Valentino watching their every move. He loved his new family.

Acknowledgements

A big thank you to Brittany Hayes for the excellent cover photography and my author photo. The model featured on the cover is our Yorkie, Wonderland's Little Miss Scarlett Ida Clair, who we usually just call Miss Scarlett.

My undying appreciation and gratitude goes out to my friends, family, and readers for their support and encouragement. A special thanks to my family for putting up with me through all my endeavors: my grandparents, Bobby and Edna Brown; my parents, Tommy and Jan Cole; my husband, Barry; and my children, Amanda, Brittany, Tyler, and baby Sophie. Y'all made me the person I am, heaven help you, and are at least partially to blame for my twisted sense of humor.

About the Author

Photo courtesy of Brittany Hayes

Tina D.C. Hayes writes romantic suspense and cozy mysteries with a paranormal twist. She lives down a little country road in western Kentucky with her husband and four children. A few pampered pooches and two parrots keep her company while they stand guard against writer's block. In her spare time she reads, hangs out with friends and family, watches movies, plays guitar, and indulges her inner Foodie in the kitchen and by chowing down at cool restaurants. Currently up to her elbows in diapers, she's an expert at 4 a.m. bottle feedings and Patty Cake.

Contact Links

Website:
http://tinadchayes.wordpress.com

Facebook:
https://www.facebook.com/TinaDCHayesAuthor

Twitter:
https://twitter.com/Tina_DC_Hayes

Books by Tina D.C. Hayes

Rock Candy Romantic Suspense
Nefarious
Harlie's whirlwind romance with a rock star pisses off a jealous stalker hell-bent on having the object of his obsession all to himself.

Petal Pushers Mystery Series
Poison, Perennials, and a Poltergeist
Darci Shelton has just one year to make her new flower shop a success, but she must come to terms with the store's resident ghost while struggling to put Petal Pushers in the black.

Secrets, Snapdragons, and a Spirit
Darci tries to help a woman reclaim her rightful name and inheritance by uncovering dark family secrets someone may have killed for. Miss Addie is

eager to help, but a ghost can only do so much.

Grudges, Goldenrods, and Ghosts

An old cookie tin buried in the cellar under Petal Pushers leads Darci to a secret someone intends to keep hidden forever.

Novellas
No More Tears

Lisa must overcome her protective instincts after her sister is sentenced to death by cancer and focus on helping her enjoy the short time she has left.

Short Stories
"Midnight Reveille"

Lily doesn't understand what's going on when she wakes up to find an unexpected visitor in her room in the middle of the night.

www.ingramcontent.com/pod-product-compliance
Lightning Source LLC
Chambersburg PA
CBHW070925130626
46555CB00001B/291